Naomi

His Protectors

Book 4

By

Ronna M. Bacon

ISBN 978-1-998821-09-9

Deuteronomy 31:6 Be strong and of a good courage, fear not, nor be afraid of them: for the LORD your God, he it is that does go with you; he will not fail you, nor forsake you.

Psalms 139:5 You have hedged me behind and before, and laid Your hand upon me.

NKJV

Table of Contents

Wandering through a small store in a town next to the one where she lived, Naomi Nasmith was bored. She was also very tired. The adventures that three of her friends from the security team that they served on had worn her out. She prayed that she and their boss, Richard, escape those adventures. Yet, somehow, she didn't think that they would. Her golden blond curls moved as she shook her head. She wasn't ready to go home, yet. Naomi felt lonely, for the first time in years. Her family lived four hours away. She missed her parents, her two sisters, and her sisters' young children.

Naomi walked through the downtown area, heading for a small shop that she loved to explore. Except today, she walked past it and headed for a small tearoom situated right beside it. There were times when she had to revisit her roots, going back to the English side of her. This tearoom let her. Her clear gray eyes searched the area, feeling watched. Her senses were on alert; she just couldn't see anyone.

Finding her favourite table empty, Naomi headed that way, waving at the owner as she did so. She sat, knowing what she wanted to order and knowing the owner, Maggie, would just bring what she usually bought. She watched the people around her. Part of her interest in people was because of her work. The other part was that she was genuinely interested in people. Her eyes stopped on a man who sat nearby. She frowned. He seemed too interested in her.

Naomi buttered her scone, reaching for the raspberry jam to drop a dollop on top of the butter. Biting into it, her eyes closed as the taste filled her mouth, bringing back memories of her grandmother's baking.

"Excuse me. You're alone. I'm moving over to sit you. A lady shouldn't be eating on her own." The harsh voice startled her.

Naomi's eyes flew open as she jumped. She turned her gaze on the man, a hardened look in his eyes.

"No, I'm fine. I want to be on my own. Thank you." Naomi memorized as many details about him as she could, something that she had been well trained to do.

"No, I don't think so." The man shoved back his chair, rising to his feet. He stopped as a younger man approached Naomi, an arm coming around her shoulders, and a kiss dropped to her cheek.

"I'm sorry, darling. I missed you in the bookstore. Somehow, I knew that I'd find you here." He slid into the chair backing to the man's table, his hand reaching for Naomi's, a squeeze seeming to ask her to play along with him.

Naomi studied him for a moment, taking in the curls that she could only describe as mahogany as well as the amber eyes. She smiled, not quite sure what to say, but willing to let the man have a chance.

"I couldn't find you either. I knew that you would track me down. Now, Maggie here will want to

—

know if you want your usual or the house special." Naomi smiled up at Maggie, finding Maggie watching the man who had approached Naomi. "Maggie?"

Maggie's attention came back to Naomi before she looked at her companion.

"Nollan Nesbitt. You and Naomi Nasmith do make a cute couple. Every one of us knows that. And Nollan, I do know your usual. It will only take a few moments."

Naomi shifted on her chair. She didn't do what she just did. She didn't let strangers hold her hand, as Nollan was now doing once more, or kiss her cheek. She stared down at her plate, praying that she had not made a mistake. Somehow, she could feel God's presence with her. She sensed that he had provided a protector for her, just as He had for others.

"Naomi?" Nollan's voice was low. "I'm sorry if I stepped in if I shouldn't have."

"No, it's okay. I just didn't want to create a scene and disturb Maggie's customers. Thank you. Maggie introduced us, I think, in her own way." She grinned as Nollan began to laugh.

"She did. Maggie's my aunt, in case you're wondering. I think that she has spoken about you to me. You're from Elmton?"

Naomi was surprised that Maggie had.

"I'm sorry. I don't know that she should have."

Nollan grinned, his smile infectious.

"I hope it's okay. She doesn't do it very often. It's just that we live in the same town. Elmton, I believe, and go to the same church. I've seen you there."

"You do? You have?" Naomi was at a loss for words, something that rarely happened. She watched as the older man rose and then walked from the tearoom, standing on the sidewalk outside, his gaze fastened on Naomi.

"He's not leaving, Naomi. I don't want you to walk away from here on your own." He looked at her in shock as she began to laugh.

"Obviously your aunt has not told you what I do for a living?" Amusement lit up her face, leaving Nollan to stare at her, entranced by her beauty. "I work for a security team. You know, those people who protect others?"

Nollan began to laugh as well, his teeth showing white against his neatly-trimmed reddish beard.

"No, she didn't give me that tidbit. And I gather that she has never talked about me?"

Naomi shook her head, trying to hide her smile. He was fishing to see if Maggie ever had, and they both knew that.

She continued to laugh, before she reached for her tea cup.

"I guess that's a no. And just what do you do? I mean, I should know right?"

"Me? My job is hard to explain. My degree is in health. But I have branched out to help with the police forces in the area when they need that kind of information."

"That sounds like a fascinating occupation." Naomi reached for her check, finding Nollan's hand there first.

"It's my treat, Naomi." He was on his feet, his hand reaching for her, before he headed for the kitchen. He knew that the man was still out there.

"We're heading the wrong way." Naomi tried to free her hand, finding Nollan's grasp just tightened on hers.

"No, it's okay. That man is still out there on the sidewalk. If we head out this way, I'll walk you to your car. I have a ride coming for me later. So I have the time."

"You do? Then, thank you." Naomi paused. She watched as he said goodbye to his aunt, seeing the resemblance between them.

Nollan reached for her hand again, walking with her towards where she had parked She stopped beside her car, her eyes on him.

"You said that you're waiting for a ride?"

Nollan nodded, reluctant to let her walk away from him. He felt the danger that she was in and wanted to protect her.

"I can give you a ride back to Elmton, if you like." Naomi offered this, knowing full well that this was not something that she would normally have done.

Nollan studied her and then the area around them. Something was off. God was nudging him to move, to get away from the car. He grabbed at her hand, pulling her with him, taking off on a run. Naomi gave a small scream, tried to free her hand, and then just ran with him.

The explosion lit up the late afternoon, Naomi's car disappearing in a ball of fire and smoke. The force of the explosion hit them like a heavy hammer to their backs, throwing them forward. Nollan grabbed for Naomi in a desperate manner, his only thought was that he needed to protect her. Their bodies slammed into the grass near the parking lot before they laid still, unmoving, as the smoke drifted their way.

Shouts and yells for help echoed through the air, some men racing for the car, fire extinguishers in hand, desperate to put out the fire, afraid that someone was in the car. Others ran for Nollan and Naomi, hands out to assess them even as the sounds of sirens split the air. Maggie was running towards her nephew, dropping to her knees, reaching to try and turn him over. He roused somewhat, his only question was that Naomi was there and okay. Naomi was not moving.

Chapter 2

Richard walked rapidly into the hospital in Elmton. He had been called by Naomi's parents that she had been injured. Would he go and be with her? They were on their way but it would take time for them to arrive. He worried about his team. Three of them had been through some rough stuff. He had prayed that Naomi would be spared. He found the charge nurse and then headed for the examination room that she pointed towards.

Standing at Naomi's bedside, Richard studied his friend, for friend was what she was. He winced at the bruising and once more prayed that she had not suffered any real injuries. But even he knew that soft tissue injuries could have devastating and long-term effects. He turned as he heard footsteps.

Bill Buckley, lead detective for the Elmton police department, walked into the room, a question on his face. He approached Richard, his eyes shifting from Richard to Naomi.

"Richard? What happened? I was called in. The patrol officers from the county asked that I did. The county is investigating as well."

Richard shrugged, his eyes back on his friend. Naomi was not moving, her face pale. He could see the scrapes on her cheek where she had landed on the ground.

"I was called by her parents. They wanted someone with her who could communicate between them and the hospital staff. I do have medical power of attorney for her, just because of where she lives and our occupation."

"She was in Oakley today?"

"She was. It's Saturday and we all scatter to do our own things. She goes there quite often. It's her place to destress."

Bill nodded, knowing that he would need to come back to speak with her.

"What have they said for injuries?"

"Probably a concussion. Bumps and bruises. Scrapes. Nothing broken. Her right wrist is sprained." Richard turned to face Bill. "I have no idea why her car exploded. That's what I'm told happened. Is she off on one of those adventures?"

Bill gave a quick grin.

"I have no idea. Do you?" He turned slightly as he heard shuffling footsteps and a man appeared who neither of them recognized.

Nollan carefully made his way to Naomi, a hand out to grip hers. Naomi moved slightly, her eyes flickering before she returned the grip. Richard and Bill stared at one another and then at Naomi.

Bill's badge was out as he moved to stand beside Nollan.

"I'm Detective Buckley from the force here. And you would be?"

Nollan looked around, surprised to see Richard and Bill there. He had been so focused on Naomi when he entered.

"I'm Nollan Nesbitt. I was with Naomi this afternoon. Is she okay?" He turned back to Naomi, not watching the other two men.

Richard and Bill exchanged another glance. This was not what they had expected. They knew that Naomi was not dating, never dated in fact.

Naomi has awakened, her eyes searching for someone. She felt the strong grip on her hand and turned that way. She blinked rapidly, her focus slowly returned. She stared at the clasped hands before her eyes raised to Nollan. She found him watching her, a look on his face that had her frowning at him.

"Nollan? You're okay? What happened?"

"I'm fine. Shaken up. Bumps and bruises. What about you?"

"The same except my wrist is sprained. And I don't know how I will work." She blinked back tears, surprising the two men with her who knew her best. She turned her head slowly as she heard a throat clear. "Richard? What are you doing here? You're not working today."

"Your mom and dad called me. They're on their way." Richard stood, arms folded across his chest.

"They did? Of course they would. I want out of here."

"Bill's here. He needs to talk with you." Richard pointed at Bill.

"He does? Bill, I don't know what happened. I had tea with Nollan. We were walking towards my car. He was catching a ride with me back here. Then, we were running away from it." Naomi frowned at Nollan. "You pulled me away from there. Why?"

"That man? The one who wanted to sit with you? By the time we were walking towards your car, I saw him leaving. I didn't get a good feeling about it and just decided that we needed to call in someone. That's why I pulled you away."

"Thank you. God put you there, I think. I needed someone there." She pushed herself upright, her eyes on Richard. "Richard, I need a ride home, seeing as I have no car. And Nollan needs a ride too. Bill, I don't know anything else."

"But you see, Naomi, you do. Nollan here just commented on a man stalking you. You need to give me a description and what happened with him."

"Actually, Bill, I don't. I need to give that to the county force. They can communicate with you if necessary." Naomi slid off the bed, towards Nollan. His hands were out to hold her steady before he simply reached for one of hers and walked away.

Bill stared after, finally remembering to snap his mouth shut. He heard Richard give a low laugh.

"You think this is funny?" Bill glared at Richard, who was a close friend and somewhat of a colleague.

"I do, Bill. It's not often that you can be told off, not by Naomi." Richard shook his head, a grin still on his face. "Give her until tomorrow. She'll calm down and talk with you. You know that."

"I do. Now, what about this Nollan? Do you know him?"

Richard nodded, a smile still hovering on his face.

"I do, in fact. We've worked on a security detail when I helped Don on my own. He's a health and safety engineer and was helping to solve a question that the investigating officer had. He's good. I don't know that he would remember me. I kept to the background, letting Don deal with him. I have no idea how these two met up, but I know that God was there. He had to be. Call her tomorrow, Bill. Or call me. I'm heading for her place. I have no idea where Nollan is heading but I would suspect somewhere that he'll be with Naomi."

Bill groaned, looking up before his eyes closed. *No, it can't be,* he thought. *Haven't we had enough of this, Lord? How many more of our friends will go through this?*

"Are you saying that Naomi is off on one of those adventures? The ones that were to stop with Stephen?"

Richard began to laugh harder, walking from the room and followed by Bill, who just kept shaking his head. Naomi turned to watch him, her eyes narrowed at his laughter.

"Sorry, Naomi. Bill just asked if you were off on one of those adventures?"

Naomi groaned, her hand tightening on Nollan's without realizing it.

"They were to stop with Stephen, weren't they?"

Richard's laughter deepened as he pointed towards his truck. With Naomi and Nollan tucked inside, he sobered somewhat.

"Yeah, one of those. Bill really does want to speak with you."

Naomi sighed.

"I know that he does. And he'll want to interrogate Nollan as well. We need to be there when he does that."

Nollan was puzzled at her last comment.

"And why would you need to do that?"

"Because he'll grill you on your intentions towards Naomi. He tends to be a bit protective of our lady friends." Richard laughed as Naomi snorted. "He is, you know."

"I know. He needs to stop." She shifted to stare at Nollan. "Nollan? Where can we drop you off?"

"Wherever you're heading. You can't be alone. You might have a concussion." It was Nollan's turn to smirk even as Richard began to laugh again.

"He's got you there, Naomi. We'll head for your place. Nollan, I have some clothes in a bag in the back there. We're about the same size. They're brand new. I'm sure that Naomi will let you clean up."

"That I will. What time do Mom and Dad get in?"

"Likely in a couple of hours. She'll smother you and then your dad will."

"That's what I'm afraid of." Naomi's voice sounded glum.

Chapter 3

Nollan hesitated as he walked towards Naomi's kitchen, looking around. He liked her home, a rambling bungalow. It was painted in a soft yellow with cream trim an dark wood floors. It was comfortable, he decided, a place where you could relax and refresh one's self.

Naomi was waiting for him, extending a mug of tea. She nodded towards the living room. Her parents were almost there. She had heard from her sisters who had been terrified for her. She was the youngest of the three, and they tried to take care of her even though she was now an adult.

Naomi curled up in her favourite chair, watching as Nollan sat on the couch, at the end near her. Richard was working in the kitchen, coming up with a light meal for them.

"You're sure that you're okay, Nollan? I'm told that you took the brunt of the fall."

"I did. It's what gentlemen do. At least, I think it is." He grinned as she shook a finger at her, a smile on her face. "I wouldn't have done anything differently, Naomi. Did you talk with an officer from there?"

"I did. It was a bomb. They don't think it was meant to go off before I was in the car. Something triggered it. Your gut feeling is what saved us. You got us out of there. That's supposed to be my job."

Nollan grinned, seeing Richard was standing there and grinning as well.

"I know. But do you have any enemies? I sure that you've made them, given what your work is."

"I may have. That's something that Richard will have us looking at on Monday." She sighed, knowing that her body would start to hurt more and more as each hour passed. She just didn't know how that she would work.

"We'll work around how you're feeling, Naomi. You know that." Richard set down the tray that was in his hands, soup and sandwiches for them on it. "Your mom called. They've been delayed by construction and will grab a bit to eat. She said that she tried to reach you."

"Did she? I left my phone on the desk in my office. I'll need to get it. Eventually. Right now, I'm not moving."

Richard grinned at her before he began to pray for her and Nollan. He was afraid that she was going to face what Timothy, Silver, and Stephen had faced. That scared him to say the least.

"Nollan? What exactly do you do?" Richard was not asking for mere curiosity. This man was unknown to them. He just needed facts to prove that he was not at fault.

"I'm a health and safety engineer. But I told Naomi that I do help the police if they need it, working with what I know. That does happen at times."

"I'm sure that it does." Richard bit into his sandwich, his eyes trained on the floor. "Something has to have triggered this, Naomi. I want to know why."

"Nor more than I do." Naomi was growing angry and tamped that down. God did allow anger, she knew, but she had to let Him have it. "Richard, I need some of your prayers. Can we do that?"

Richard nodded, knowing that Naomi did indeed need those. He simply bowed his head and prayed. It didn't matter to him that his soup would grow cold. His friend was more important. He was not surprised to hear Nollan pick up the petition. He frowned for a moment, wondering just how well these two knew one another. It appeared that they had been friends for years.

Naomi was on her feet an hour later, heading for the door. She had heard a key in the lock and knew that her parents had arrived. Eve looked up from removing her shoes and simply reached to hug her daughter. Benjamin moved in on his ladies, wrapping them both in a hug, praying for his daughter.

Richard was on his feet, a hand extended to Benjamin and then hugging Eve. He had gotten to know this couple over the years and appreciated them so much. Nollan stood uncertainly, not sure what to do or what to say.

Naomi reached to wrap an arm around his, her hand finding his. Their eyes met and Nollan frowned for a moment. Somehow, he didn't think this was normal for her.

Eve and Benjamin hesitated for a moment until Naomi introduced them. Then, Eve reached to hug the man standing with her daughter. Benjamin reached for his hand and then simply hugged the younger man. Words could not express their gratitude that he had saved their daughter.

"Mom. Dad. This is Nollan. He's the one who pulled me away from my car. Nollan. These are my parents, Eve and Benjamin."

"Thank you, son." Benjamin had trouble getting out the words. He turned away for a moment, finding Richard next to him and drawing him away.

Eve watched the interaction between the two. She frowned for a moment. She didn't recognize Nollan or his name. How had they met? She could question her daughter but she was not sure that she would receive an answer. Naomi had learned to keep quiet her life.

Nollan hesitated once more. He needed to head for home. Only he had no transportation. He sat back down where he had been, watching Naomi for a moment. She in turn watched him before she excused herself and sat beside him.

"Nolan?"

"I need to go home, Naomi. Only I don't have my car." Nollan refused to look at her.

"No, you're staying here tonight, Nollan. You need to. You were unconscious until you roused in the hospital. I promised that you would not be on your own. Do you have someone to stay with you?"

Nollan shook his head, sorrow in his heart for a moment.

"No, I don't. I don't have family in town. I'll be okay."

Naomi's arms were around him as she hugged him. She heard her mother moving closer to them before she sat on the coffee table. Eve's eyes were on Nollan as she tried to control her emotions.

"We'll be your family, Nollan. At least for the night. Naomi has plenty of room. In fact, I would say that the room that you used earlier is yours for the night. Her father and I are here until Monday. Richard has left. So please, stay."

Nollan looked at her before looking up at Benjamin. His face and mouth worked with his emotions for a moment before he gave a nod, unable to express his thanks. He felt as if he now had a family. Only, that shouldn't be. He had just met them.

Chapter 4

The next morning, Naomi was on the move early in the morning. She has spoken to her sisters and reassured them that she was fine and that she didn't need them to come. She was grateful that they were all close. Naomi paused for a moment as she passed Nollan's room, a prayer of thankfulness raised that he had been there yesterday. She not likely would have been here today except for his quick actions.

Starting the coffee for her father and plugging in the kettle for the rest of them, Naomi turned to the outside. She needed that time alone, she knew, just to spend time with her heavenly Father.

Nollan stopped in the kitchen, pouring his mug of coffee and making a cup of tea for Naomi. He headed for the back deck, looking for Naomi. He set their mugs down and then walked down the steps towards her.

Naomi turned as she heard his whistle. He reached to hug her, finding her hugging him back. They turned and walked the yard, no conversation between them. Nollan reached for her hand, leading her back to the porch. Naomi sat, her eyes on Nollan. He was treating her as a lady who he wanted in his life. She didn't understand that. Nollan didn't realize that he was under such deep scrutiny. He instead began to pray for her and her situation.

Benjamin stood at the back door. He had opened it, intending on finding his daughter. He paused as he heard Nollan's prayer. He stepped back, finding Eve beside him, a puzzled look on her face.

"Benjamin? Aren't you going outside?"

"I am but Nollan is praying for Naomi. I won't intrude."

"Do we know him? I don't remember hearing Naomi speak of him."

"I don't think that we do. I had a chance to speak with Richard last night as he was leaving. He doesn't know much about him as well. Knowing Richard, he'll have done a search of him."

"I'm sure that he will have." Eve glanced at the clock. "We're staying until tomorrow?"

"We are, unless Naomi wants us to leave today."

Eve moved away to start their breakfast.

Benjamin turned as he heard the doorbell and walked that way. He opened it to find Bill standing there.

"Bill? What are you doing are?"

"Looking for Naomi. Is she here?" Bill stepped into the house.

"She is. She's on the back porch. Nollan is still here as well."

"He is? Good. I need to speak with him as well."

"First, we eat. Then, we pray. You know our routine, Bill." Benjamin was a counsellor with a Christian firm.

"Sounds like a plan. I was up all night at a crime scene." He stared at Naomi as Naomi entered the kitchen, Nollan on her heels. "Naomi? We need to speak."

"We do, Bill. As long as it's quick. We have church this morning and I need to be there. I'm on the worship team this morning."

"We'll do what we can. Nollan? How are you feeling this morning?" Bill eyed the other man, not sure why he was there.

"I'm hurting, Bill. Jus as you would expect. Naomi and her folks were kind enough to have me stay here overnight, just as was asked by the physician that I not be on my own. I'm heading home this morning. Benjamin has been kind enough to offer to drop me off."

Nollan walked away, leaving Bill staring after him. Naomi strode up to him, anger sparking for a moment before she calmed herself down.

"Leave him alone, Bill. He saved my life yesterday. I consider him a friend now."

"I'm sorry, Naomi. You are correct. I apologize to you. Nollan will get one too. It's just that three of your team have been through danger. I don't want to see you hurt."

"It's past that point, Bill. I have been. Now, we have to determine why. And I don't know where to start. Do you?" Naomi was challenging him. Both of them knew that.

Bill shook his head, a small grin lurking on his face. Naomi was correct. They did have to determine that. *Lord, I could use some help here. Once more, one of my friends is in danger from someone. We don't know who or why. Protect this friend of mine. And protect Nollan as well. I need to speak with him. Only for once, I'm not sure of the words.*

Nollan had his eye on Bill, knowing that Bill had suspicions about him. He would sit down with him and be honest with him. That's all that he could do. He turned as he felt a hand on his arm, Naomi standing there, a question on her face.

Andrew McBeth stood later that morning, his eyes on Naomi. Bill had been in touch with him, knowing that as the police chief, Andrew would need to be aware of what had happened. Andrew had shaken his head, asked for details, and then turned to find Naomi. She was avoiding him, he decided. He would find her later. He simply reached for his young daughter who lunged at him from his wife's arm.

Richard watched Naomi as well, assessing how she was. He sighed. They were right, he decided. His team members had been certain that Stephen was not the last one of them to face this kind of danger.

Timothy and Tate stopped beside Naomi, Timothy with a frown on his face. He raised his eyes to Nollan before nodding. He knew Nollan from a Bible study group that they were both in. He just didn't know how he connected with Naomi.

"Naomi?" Tate's soft voice caught Naomi's attention. "Are you all right?"

Naomi nodded, realizing that Nollan still held her hand even though the service had ended. Naomi had been seated between Nollan and her mother during the service, his hand reaching for hers at every opportunity. Her parents had exchanged a glance at one point before her father shrugged. Benjamin had been able to have a good talk with Nollan the night before, and he was satisfied that Nollan only wanted the best for his youngest daughter.

"I think so. I hurt, as you would expect me to." She looked up at Nollan to find his gaze on her. "Nollan was hurt too."

Timothy stared at her.

"What do you mean, Naomi? Richard said that your car explode."

"It did. If Nollan had not been there, I wouldn't have survived. For some reason, he pulled me away from it." Naomi was puzzled by how Nollan had known there was something wrong.

"Nollan?" Timothy's voice had Nollan turning to him. "How did you know?"

"God. I saw the man who had tried to intimidate and threaten Naomi in my aunt's tea room. He was near her car. I just didn't have a good feeling about it. I had planned to call in the police but the car exploded before I could."

Timothy stared at Nollan and then at Naomi. He had not expected to hear that. He looked up to see Stephen and Silver standing nearby, shock on their faces.

Chapter 5

Naomi walked into their office building the next morning, a sigh rising from her. She really didn't want to be there. Her parents had set off for home, and she missed them already. She had received a text from Nollan, just to say good morning.

Richard was right behind her, his eyes assessing her and her fitness for work. She was due in for training their client team that morning on how to source out safe houses for the people that they were hired to protect. Richard's security team used to do that until Richard had switched to a niche area, that of training.

"Naomi?" Richard waited patiently for Naomi to speak.

Naomi jumped, not having heard Richard's footsteps behind her. She spun, her purse and keys falling to her desk top with a soft jingle.

"I didn't hear you, Richard. I'm sorry."

Richard shrugged. His thoughts turned to prayer for his team mate and friend.

"It's okay, Naomi. You didn't expect anyone here." Richard moved past her, dropping his briefcase in his office and then heading for the conference room. The trainees were due in later, but first, his team would meet for prayer and then a final discussion of the training schedule. It was what they always did.

—

Naomi frowned as she stared around her office. Something felt off. Her feelings were enough for her to start a systemic search of her office. Silver stood for a moment before she moved in to help search. Timothy and Stephen simply watched, ready to step in if needed.

"What's going on?" Richard had approached from behind them, slightly confused as to the ladies' actions.

"Something is off in here, Richard." Naomi yanked open the drawers on the lateral filing cabinet, her hand running over the drawers. "I just feel it."

Richard's face grew grim. A quiet word to the other two men had them on the move. Both Timothy and Stephen began a search of the office. Richard headed for the computer that was locked in a small office. He pulled up the security system app and scrolled through it. He paused it at a point during the night. Richard sat back before he reached for his phone.

"Bill? Richard. We had a security breach over night. We're searching the building. It seems as if it might be concentrated in Naomi's office."

Bill rose, heading for Andrew, knowing that Richard was likely correct. Andrew's head raised from his desk work, standing as Bill beckoned to him.

"Bill? What's going on?"

"Richard called. They've had a breach at their office. He thinks that it's related to what happened to

Naomi on Saturday. She's tearing apart her office." Bill headed for his vehicle, Andrew beside him.

Naomi spun in a circle. Her office was clear but she felt that someone had been in there. Her eyes narrowed as they raised to the ceiling.

"Timothy? We have a ladder, correct?" Her voice brought him back to her office.

"We do. Why?" He followed her line of sight to the acoustic tiles before he was away and back with a ladder. He had unfolded it and was climbing it as Richard approached, Bill and Andrew in tow.

"Timothy? Is there a reason for the ladder?" Richard was somewhat puzzled.

"There is. Naomi's office is clear but they could have hidden something up here." He reached for the flashlight that Stephen extended to him. He shone it around, the beam stopping at a point just within his reach. He sighed, his hand reaching for the device. Timothy handed it down to Stephen who in turn handed it to Richard. "That's the only one I can see here, but we will need to search the entire area." He was down off the ladder, folding it to head for another office.

Richard turned the device over and over in his hands. He had not seen anything like that. It was sophisticated, he would grant the intruder that.

Bill slapped on latex gloves and took it from Richard. He too studied it, raising it to look at it closely.

—

32

"It's similar to microphones that you would find on hearing aids. Very new to the trade, I think. Richard? Where is your security feed?" Bill followed Richard, heading for the locked room.

Andrew stayed where he was, listening to Naomi and Silver speaking. Naomi stood with her eyes on him, knowing full well that he wanted to speak with her.

"Andrew?" Naomi walked towards him as Silver headed out of the building and for the training centre. She was needed there as was Timothy.

"Naomi? What have you gone and done? Don't you remember that it was to stop with Stephen?" He simply grinned at her.

Naomi began to laugh, grateful for her friends. She also began to pray for herself and her team mates and also Nollan. This was only to get worse, she knew.

"It was. This does not mean that I'm going through anything." She shook a finger at her friend, finding him sobering. "Andrew? It doesn't. That was an unusual event on Saturday"

Andrew was shaking his head. He reached out to gently lead her to the kitchen area, shoving her down. He turned to make her a cup of tea and poured himself a mug of coffee. Setting the mugs on the table, he drew back a chair and sat. He prayed for his friend and for the words that were needed

"It's not a single event, Naomi. I think that you suspect that. Bill will be speaking with you later. However, I do need to step in for a moment. We

—

received the report on your car. It was a bomb, Naomi, that destroyed it."

Naomi paled, her hands clenching around her mug. She had suspected as much. Nollan had questioned her the afternoon before. He had dropped some hints that maybe it wasn't just an accident.

"You sure?" She dropped her face into her hands. "Of course, you're sure. You wouldn't be saying that if you weren't."

"We are. They found evidence of it. The techs can't tell why it exploded when it did. We're looking at it as a threat towards you. We just don't know why. Bill will be asking you about your friends, your family, and anyone that you may have had a run-in with in your past. We'll be digging as deep as we can. Richard will be approached regarding your assignments. This is personal, though, Naomi. We need you to take the precautions that will protect you."

Naomi blew out a breath, knowing that Andrew was right. Her freedom has just walked away. *Scrap that,* she thought. *My freedom didn't walk away. It just got up and ran away from me as fast as it could.*

Andrew watched with compassion at the emotions flickered across her face. He was well aware of the danger that she faced. He and Phoebe had been through something similar. He wished it on no one.

Chapter 6

Nollan turned from his work late that afternoon. He stared down at his computer and then simply saved what he was working on. It was not yet quitting time. He had had enough for the day. His body ached and so did his heart. Naomi had become a part of his friend list, and he felt worried for her.

Walking out of his building after securing it behind him, Nollan's footsteps slowed. He didn't recognize the woman who was waiting for him, but her very bearing shouted law enforcement.

"Nollan Nesbitt? I'm Detective Lily Gordon. I just need to speak with you about what happened on Saturday." Lily's identification was out as Nollan's footsteps slowed and stopped. "Do you have a few moments?"

"I do. I can open my office up again." Nollan started to turn, stopping as Lily spoke.

"No, that's fine. There's a coffee shop across the road. If you have the time, we can grab a coffee. I know that I could use one." Lily grinned at him, bringing an answering smile to his face.

"That works." Nollan walked beside her, held the door open for her, and then simply paid for their coffees. He sat, his eyes on Lily, his face noncommittal in emotion.

"May I call you Nollan?" Lily waited for his nod before she continued. "I needed just to speak with you regarding what happened on Saturday. It's just part of our normal follow up to it."

Nollan had expected it, curious as to what she would ask him.

"Okay, then. Walk me through your day up to that point." Lily had her notepad out and her pen ready.

"Where do you want me to start?" Nollan was not ready to speak, not sure if he was a suspect or not. "You suspect me of planting the bomb."

"No, we don't. And how did you know that it was a bomb?" Lily and Bill had spoken about that. Not knowing Nollan, they had decided that they needed to speak with him about that. Lily had been digging into his background, surprised to find out his occupation and the numerous awards that he had already received given he wasn't much older than she was.

"I've been in places where these things happen, Detective. It is not something that you forget. I've been out on short mission trips to countries where this is part and parcel of daily life. You learn quickly to trust your instincts. And if God tells you to run, you run. You ask why afterwards."

"And this is what happened here." Lily had no doubt that he would say that it was.

"It was, Detective. Having been close to one that exploded, I never wanted to be that close again. I can't explain totally why I felt like I did. It was the man standing there that triggered some warning. I was in my Aunt Maggie's tea room, saw him making the moves on Naomi, and could see that she was uncomfortable. I didn't think. I just moved in and sat with her. Aunt Maggie had talked about her, describe her, and made me feel as if I knew her. She didn't shove me away and say no. I know what she does for a living. Sometimes those who are the protectors need protecting themselves."

Lily's eyes were steady on him as he spoke. She nodded at his last statement. That was the character of the man that she had been investigating.

"Have you ever seen this man before?"

Nollan shook his head.

"No, I haven't. But I was able to snap a photo of him that afternoon. I can print it off for you or send it to you, whichever you prefer." Nollan's phone was out as he found the photo. He took Lily's business card and forwarded the photo.

Lily studied it, a frown on her face. Her heart tightened. This man was known to them. He was wanted in many jurisdictions. They all wanted him arrested but so far, he had been eluding arrest. He was a hit man for hire.

"You look disturbed, Detective." Nollan had been watching her closely.

"I am. I know of this man. God had His hand on you two on Saturday. Anything else to add?"

Nollan shook his head, feeling that Lily had picked his brain clean

"Not that I can think of. If you wonder why I wasn't driving? My car was having work done on it that day. A cousin had picked me up and taken me there. He was going to drive me home. It's what we do. He may be my cousin but he is also a close friend."

Lily nodded before she read back through her notes. Nollan had been open and honest with her. She just felt as if she was missing something. She just didn't know that that something was.

"Thank you for your time, Nollan. I have your contact information if I need more information. I more than likely will be speaking with you again about this. Or Bill will." She rose, her eyes on him. "Naomi is a close friend of ours. That makes no difference in how we investigate. We don't want to see her hurt." Lily walked away, leaving Nollan staring out of the window in front of him.

He sat for a while, not noticing that his coffee had grown cold. He heard a voice speaking with him. He looked around to find Richard standing there, fresh cups of coffee in hand.

"Nollan? How are you?" Richard sat, eying the man in front of him.

Nollan shrugged, not sure why Richard was there. He studied him, a question on his face.

"I was stopping in for coffee. I had been doing business in the area. I didn't want to intrude when Lily was speaking with you."

Nollan shrugged, hearing the question in Richard's voice.

"It's okay. I just feel as if I'm a suspect."

Richard laughed, bringing a sheepish fire to Nollan's face.

"They make you feel like that.   It's not intentional. They just have to do what they have to do." Richard was unsure what to say.

"You want to ask something, Richard. What is it?" Nollan took pity on him.

"I do. Naomi has told us what happened from her perspective. She said that she hadn't met you before but was grateful that you stepped in."

"That was my aunt's tea room. Aunt Maggie has talked to both of us over time about the other. Maybe just talking but knowing Aunt Maggie, she may have been trying her hand at matchmaking." Nollan gave a brief grin at Richard's laugh. "Yeah, she does that. But what was it that you wanted to know?"

"The man. Naomi didn't know him but felt real evil from him." Richard didn't quite know how to express what he wanted to ask.

"I didn't either, Richard. He just had such a sense of evil from him. I agree with her. I couldn't step back and not help out a lady. That's not how I always felt that I should be raised."

"Should be? What do you mean?"

"I mean that I was raised by parents who were great. I was closer to Aunt Maggie than my other relatives. They were killed in a car accident when I was nineteen. I miss them and would love for them to be here my life."

—

"Listen, Nollan. You're going to be in our lives from now on. We would like to consider you a friend needing our help. Let me have what information you have on your family. We'll look into it. I also have a friend or two that can help." Richard's smile hid his emotions as he watched Nollan's face work as he tried to control himself.

"Thank you, Richard. That means a lot." Nollan stared at his phone. "May I have your phone number? I have a photo of the man. I can forward it to you."

Chapter 7

Naomi peeked through the side window of her front door, not expecting anyone that evening. She had planned to relax. She was hurting all over, more than she had been on the day before. Frowning, she reached to unlock the door and then push open the storm door.

"Nollan? You're here?" She stepped back to let him in. She frowned at the bags in his hand.

Nollan grinned, holding up the bags.

"I brought a meal. If you won't eat with me, I'll leave your share and leave you in peace. I just know that I didn't feel like cooking for myself tonight."

"I didn't either. I was probably not going to eat." Naomi grinned at him, his infectious smile irresistible. "What did you bring?"

"Burgers and fries. Soft drinks. I hope that was okay. I asked for the toppings on the side. Ev was going to oblige me until she heard it was for you. She assured me that she knew what you liked."

"She does." Naomi headed for the kitchen, pointing to the table. "Here. Thank you, Nollan. This is so sweet of you."

Nollan shrugged, thinking that it was Naomi was sweet. He reached for her hand as he bowed his head to ask the blessing on their food. Naomi had jumped as his hand found hers and then relaxed. *Is he the one, Lord? Is he the one who You have planned for me? I don't want to ruin a friendship. Guard our hearts and words, dear Lord. Protect this friend of mine.*

Nollan gathered up their garbage when their meal was finished and dropped it into the garbage can. He nodded as Naomi held up the coffee pot. He was in no rush to leave but he would have to soon.

Naomi led the way to the outdoors, finding a seat on the porch steps. This was a favourite spot of hers. Nollan sat beside her, his hands wrapping around his mug.

"Nollan? How was your day?" Naomi waited for him to speak.

"It was okay. I'm deep into an investigation for someone. But I had a conversation with a detective named Lily."

"Lily? She tracked you down, did she?" Naomi grinned at him. "Don't worry. She's a friend. If you were a true suspect, she would tell you that."

Nollan drew a pretend sigh of relief, grinning at her.

"I was worried for a moment. It's good to know that. Richard had coffee with me afterwards. He said that he had been in the neighbourhood."

Naomi frowned and then her face cleared.

"Where's your office?" When he told her, she nodded. "He had some things to drop off at the homeless shelter today. That's near there." Naomi grew quiet, content just to sit beside Nollan. She didn't need conversation although there was that.

———

Nollan walked away a short time later, his heart feeling happy for the first time in years. He enjoyed his time spent with Naomi. Her conversation could be serious. She did have a sense of humour that he respected.

He headed for his home, not seeing the lights of the vehicle that followed him. He waited for the garage door to rise and then drove in. Turning off the vehicle, he waited for a moment before he left the vehicle and headed for the door that would let him into his house. His briefcase was dropped near the door leading to the hallway. Nollan decided that he would not work any more that night. Instead, he headed up the stairs, showered, and changed into comfortable clothes. He would spend the evening in prayer and reading through the verses that God had been laying on his mind.

Richard stood for a moment, staring at his office building. He could still see it still through the growing dusk. He was concerned, he had to admit to himself, that someone had entered the building. His security was one of the best but someone had managed to get in. How did he prevent that from happening again? That was his question. He had reached out to two friends with security teams, Don and Abe, for their input. Both men had been out on assignments but had promised to be in touch as soon as they could.

Bill wearily walked towards his home. He had missed his dinner with his wife, Cora, and his young son, Michael. He was disappointed at that. There were just so many investigations, he thought. This one with Naomi? It was not what they needed. Once more, a friend was in danger but he had no idea where it would lead. All he knew was that she was in danger and he just couldn't understand that. God was in control, he had to admit, but sometimes, that didn't make it any easier.

Timothy set his phone to one side, reaching for his wife, Tate, and just wrapping her into a hug. They knew only too well what Naomi seemed to be facing. He prayed for their friend, but he was still worried.

"Timothy? What can we do to help Naomi?"

"I'm not sure, love. I'm really not sure." His chin rested on the top of her head. Three of the team were now married, changing the dynamics of life for them. Their families were first and then their security team, unless they were at work. Then they had to set aside their families and do what they were trained to do.

Lily set aside her phone at last. She had spent time speaking with Naomi, just trying to understand what had happened. Neither one of the ladies could put a finger on what happened. They just knew that God had protected Naomi that Saturday. Lily walked through the department building, a frown on her face. She needed to find that man but no one had any information absit him. That disturbed her a great deal. She and Bill were to meet in the morning before Lily headed for the nearing village, to view the scene and to speak with anyone who might have information.

Neither Nollan nor Naomi were aware of the men who patrolled outside of their homes, staying in the shadows. They also stayed far enough away that the security cameras did not pick them up. It was not the first time that they had been there. And it not likely would be the last.

The stars and moon shone brightly down on the homes. Naomi's sleep was restless and broken. She rose at last, the early dawn light just breaking the eastern sky. She reached for her Bible, needing to find the verses that she needed for that day. She was afraid. And fear was not something that was normal for her.

Chapter 8

Friday morning found Nollan running for his office door, dodging the raindrops that dropped slowly from the dark sky. He had not wanted to work that day. He had days like that. Setting his briefcase in his office, he walked through the building, heading for his work room. A sound had him turning and staring towards an empty office. He walked that way. Nollan didn't think that anyone was there.

Flicking on the overhead lights, he walked through the room. It was a storage room, holding the tools and paperwork of his trade. He had set it up himself and knew where everything should be. He turned as he reached the end of it and shook his head. He was hearing things, he decided, before he walked back towards the door.

Nollan didn't see the dark figure that had taken refuge behind the door. A small sound had him turning slightly, an arm rising to try and protect himself. It was to no avail. The pipe landed heavily on his arm before it continued to slap into his shoulder. Pain dropped Nollan to the floor. His vision darkened from it as he lost consciousness. He was sure how long he had been there when he heard voices around him. Rousing slightly, he had asked if they had his attacker. He was gone again into that deep well of darkness before he could hear the response.

The paramedics shook their heads at Bill before they were headed off with Nollan. This was not the way his day was to go, Bill thought, before he watched

—

the crime scene techs start their search. He turned then and headed for Nollan's secretary.

Maeve Brown stood there, worry on her face. She was older, nearing a time when she should retire. She had taken the work that Nollan had offered her when her husband had died. She had been refused work at so many places that she had felt despair. Nollan was a kind and compassionate boss.

"Maeve? What time would he have been in?" Bill's question steadied her nerves and had her thinking about the day.

"He would likely have been in around six. Fridays, he comes in early and then leaves early. We don't work past noon on Fridays unless we have to. And that is very rare. So it would have been about three hours or so before I found him." Maeve was worried. She had seen the pain on Nollan's face.

"Okay. Now about his work. What can you tell me?"

Maeve went on to explain what Nollan did and how it would impact the medical world. Then, she paused, her eyes troubled.

"Maeve? What aren't you saying?" Bill waited patiently for her to gather her thoughts and think.

"I can't tell you what all he was working on. That's not my place. He has to tell you. I just don't know if he's made any enemies over the years."

"He may have. If he has, he hasn't said. And I have not seen anything coming into the office." Maeve walked away, needing to deal with the work on her desk.

Bill walked towards her.

'One last question, Maeve. Who is his power of attorney for medical reasons?"

Maeve looked up. She shook her head.

"That would likely be his aunt or his cousin. His parents disappeared when he was nineteen, I think."

Bill walked away from the office building, heading for the hospital. He spoke with the physician treating Nollan. The news was not good. A broken arm and broken clavicle was the diagnosis. The pain had driven him to unconsciousness. They would need to take him to surgery to set the bones. Did Bill know who the medical power of attorney was?

Bill had walked away, looking for a number for Nollan's aunt. Maggie had been horrified to hear what had happened but agreed to speak with the surgeon. Her son, she indicated, was also his power of attorney and was actually in Elmton that morning, making deliveries for her. Maggie agreed to find him and send him that way.

Bill spoke with the physician again and then found his vehicle again. He paused, his eyes on the horizon. He would need to find Naomi, he decided. She would need to know that something had happened to Nollan. He just didn't know how the incidents were related.

Bill found Richard in the training building, watching as Naomi led the session on safe houses. He listened to her and realized how good she was at her job. He had expected nothing less than that. He pointed out the door, drawing Richard from the building.

"Bill? You need to speak with Naomi?" Richard asked the obvious question.

"I do, when's she finished."

"She'll be about thirty more minutes. Come with me. I was heading for the office, to make fresh coffee. You look as if you could use a cup or two." Richard grinned at his friend, seeing the stress in Bill's eyes that he was trying to hide.

The men spoke quietly about the Bible study that they were part of. They were studying verses about God's protection. Richard appreciated that. His team had needed that and still needed that.

Naomi paused for a moment as she saw Bill. Her work was done for the day, she knew, her notes made and filed. She walked by the two men, poured her coffee and turned. Bill shoved back a chair with his toe, nodding towards it.

"Naomi? You're done for the day?"

"I am, Bill. You're not here to find out what hours I work, I don't think. Spill. Why are you here? Have you found that man yet and solved this?"

Bill grinned at her questions, knowing full well that was Naomi.

"No, I haven't found that man. And no, it's not solved." Bill sobered, his eyes shifting between

Richard and Naomi. Richard had said the others were now teaching.

"What then?" Naomi's face paled. "Nollan?"

Bill nodded, knowing that once he spoke, Naomi would be on her feet, running for her car, and then heading to find Nollan. A quick glance at Richard had the other man, nodding, a hand reaching out to rest on Naomi's arm.

"Bill?" Naomi could feel herself beginning to panic, something that never happened to her.

"Nollan was attacked this morning in his office, Naomi. His secretary said that he is usually in around six in the morning and that she gets in about three hours later. She found him unconscious. He has a broken arm and a broken clavicle. He's facing surgery. His cousin and aunt will be with him. Has he said anything to you?"

Naomi shook her head, puzzled at Bill's question.

"No, he hasn't. Not that he would. I would have no need to know that, would I?" Naomi was on her feet, heading for her office. She wiped at her eyes, tears overcoming her for a moment before she grabbed her purse and headed for her car. She knew where she was going. She just didn't know if she would be welcomed there.

Chapter 9

Maggie turned from where she had been staring out of the window in the surgical waiting room. She was worried about her nephew. His parents had died just as he had finished high school in a horrible auto accident during a heavy rainstorm. She had taken him in at that point. They had always been close, but this shared sorrow of loss had drawn them closer.

His cousin, Michael, approached his mother, his face stern. He reached to hug her before drawing her to a chair.

"Any word yet, Mom?" Michael was hopeful.

"Not yet. There should be soon." Maggie looked around as she heard footsteps that hesitated at the entrance to the room. She was on her feet, heading for Naomi. "Naomi?"

Naomi looked up, a troubled look on her face. She walked into the older woman's hug.

"I'm sorry, Maggie. I had to come. I need to know how Nollan is." She tried to step back and move away.

Maggie simply did not let her. With an arm around her, she drew her down to a chair beside her. Michael watched silently, knowing who this was. He had not met her but his mother had described her very well.

"No, you need to be, I think, Naomi. We're waiting for word." Maggie watched the emotions

—

51

flickering across Naomi's face, knowing that this was unusual for her.

"If I could wait with you?" Naomi knew that she had no right to be there, but she had to be. She felt that this was her fault. Only, she didn't know why.

Richard had followed Naomi, worried about her. He cared about his team members. His prayer reached to the heavens, asking for protection for his friend. He nodded at Michael, a frown on his face. He knew Michael quite well, he decided. He had not realized that the other man was related to Nollan.

Michael was on his feet, reaching to shake Richard's hand.

"Richard? I didn't expect to see you." Michael looked between Naomi and Richard before understanding that Naomi must be one of his employees.

"Michael? I didn't know that Nollan was related to you."

"My cousin. We're his only family now. But I don't understand why you are here."

"Naomi's my employee and a good friend. She headed here to see what she could discover about Nollan." Richard sighed. This was getting old, he decided, with friends in danger. He had prayed that Naomi would miss this. It didn't seem as if she would.

Michael nodded, knowing that Richard was correct.

"He's hurting, I would suspect, Richard. The surgeon talked to us before heading into the operating room. He'll keep him overnight seeing as it's that late. Then, he'll head home. We just don't know how he'll manage on his own for the first few days. I have to travel next week. Mom is away on vacation." Michael was trying to find a way to help his cousin.

"He can stay with me. I have lots of room, as you know." Michael had been a guest at Richard's for a shared meal more than once, Richard opening his home to the Bible study group that they were part of.

"Thank you, Richard. That's a relief for us." Michael was watching Naomi. "She's upset"

"She is. She's still trying to work through what happened with her car. We watch for things like that all the time when we're working. Or we did. Now that we're training, we don't have that exposure." Richard grew silent, thinking back over the years, trying to come up with a name that he could pass on to Bill or Lily.

"That was strange. Nollan said it was just out of the blue. Now with his assault? Are they two connected?"

Richard shrugged. That was a question he and his other team mates had been working through. They had not found a connection. It had to be there somewhere, he knew.

"I don't know." Richard was on the move, an arm around Naomi as the surgeon approached.

"Maggie?" Wilt Walton sat beside her. His wife and he were frequent customers at her tea room.

"Wilt? You have news?" Maggie's hand reached for Naomi, keeping her in her chair. Michael and Richard moved closer.

"I do. He does have a fracture of both bones in his lower left arm. We have had to use plates and screws to repair them. The collarbone? Again a plate and some screws. He will heal and should regain complete use of that arm. That being said, he will be handicapped for a number of weeks. Once we can, we'll get him into physiotherapy."

"Thank you, Wilt. It has been a worry." Maggie chewed at her lip for a moment. "Will it affect his work?"

Wilt nodded, knowing what Maggie was asking.

"It can. I know what he does. He will need to be off work for a few days. But I know him. He won't."

"No, he won't." Michael spoke up. "We'll see what we can do."

Wilt nodded, knowing how close the cousins were.

Richard's eyes were on Naomi, who was watching him in return.

"Naomi?" Maggie's voice broke into Naomi's thoughts. "We'll get you in to see Nollan. You need that."

Naomi nodded before her eyes slid closed for a moment. She was on her feet, walking towards Richard, who backed away. He simply hugged her and then, with an arm around her shoulders, turned her away to walk the hallway.

"Naomi? Talk to me?" Richard waited patiently for her to speak.

"Is it because of me? Was Nollan hurt because of me?" Naomi's worry had only been growing over the time since she had heard about Nollan.

"We don't know, Naomi. We really don't know. It could be. And your car? That could have been because of Nollan. We just don't have the information to determine that. You know how long it can take."

"I do, unfortunately. I don't know if I can do this, Richard. With what Timothy, Silver, and Stephen went through, I should have expected this. We all should have."

"We have expected this, Naomi. We've been working on a plan. All of us have. Timothy and Stephen are working on a plan to keep you safe. That plan now includes Nollan."

Naomi nodded, stopping for a moment. She wrapped her arms around herself, just staring down the hall, not seeing the people moving through the hall. She knew that Richard stood beside her. Someone was on her left side. She just didn't know who. Michael had moved in, standing beside her. He was not in law enforcement or security, but he was willing to protect the lady who his cousin seemed interested in.

—

Chapter 10

Nollan glared at his cousin the next day. He was dressed and ready to leave, except Michael was not letting him. He needed to be in his workshop. He had investigations that he needed to complete and that had to be done today.

"I have to be in the office, Michael. I don't have a choice." He knew that his strength was limited but that would not stop him.

"Nollan? You just had surgery yesterday. You need to recover from that." Michael was frustrated with his cousin. He knew that he should have expected this. He just hadn't.

"It doesn't matter, Michael. I have to finish those investigations. Time is limited on them." Nollan was on his feet, walking towards the door. His feet stopped in their forward motion as he saw Naomi there, Richard beside her.

"Nollan? Where are you heading?" Naomi's voice, while soft, was still questioning.

"I need to head for my office. There are investigations that I need to complete. Michael here doesn't want me to."

Michael stood behind his cousin, shaking his head at Naomi and Richard.

"He has just had surgery. He needs to take today." Michael finally just raised his hands and walked away, heading for his vehicle. He needed to be somewhere for his own work. He couldn't wait for Nollan to decide where to go. *Lord, please heal my cousin. He understands that I have commitments that I need to be at. Protect him and his lady.*

Naomi linked her arm with Nollan's good one and walked with him towards the elevators. Richard nodded as he took the discharge papers. He knew that Naomi would not be returning to the office that day. It was all right with him. Nollan needed protection. For now, that would be Naomi. He would float between the training building and Naomi.

Naomi wandered through Nollan's office, an eye out for the security that he had. She nodded. His was good. She just didn't understand how the assailant had made it into the building. She would ask Timothy or Stephen to drop by on their way home and search.

Nollan's head dropped by early afternoon. He was exhausted. He had known that he was pushing it, but the investigation that he should have completed yesterday was now done. He sent it on to the company requesting it.

With a hand supporting his other arm, Nollan searched for Naomi, finding her in his office, her phone out as she worked away. She looked up with a smile. He paused, seeing in her the lady that he had had in his dreams for years. He was sure, though, that she would just walk away from him.

"All done?" Naomi was on her feet.

"I am. I just have to go through this mail and give my secretary what I need to. Then I can leave.

But I can't drive." Nollan sorted through in his mind who he could talk into driving his car to his house.

"That's not a problem, Nollan. I can do that. Stephen and Timothy are going to come through your building this afternoon and upgrade your security where it needs to be. We need to do that for you. They are also investigating how your assailant got in."

"That's what I don't understand. Bill was around early this morning. I couldn't tell him. He said that they searched and couldn't find out how. The only people with keys and the security codes are myself, my secretary, and the cleaners." He paused at the look on Naomi's face. "Naomi?"

"Your cleaners? How long have they worked for you?"

"The cleaners? A couple of years, I guess. Why?" Nollan handed off the paperwork to his secretary, reached for his briefcase, and followed Naomi out of the building.

Naomi unlocked the truck doors, watching as Nollan awkwardly climbed into the passenger seat. She made a complete circle of the vehicle once more even though she had already been out and done that. Starting up the truck, Naomi simply waited. Patience was one of her strengths.

"Naomi, you don't have to do this."

"I do. And just how are you going to manage on your own for the next while?" Naomi and Richard had talked at length about that.

Nollan gave a one-shoulder shrug. He had no idea how he would do just that. His aunt had asked him to come and stay with her. He had refused, partly because he did not want to bring any more danger to her. Michael had offered to stay with him, but Nollan had refused that offer as well. He knew the long hours that Michael was having to put in at the moment. He didn't want to stress him out even more.

"I don't know how I'll manage, but I will." Nollan stared out of the side window, watching the traffic and scenery as it passed by.

"Richard would like you to stay with him for the next few days. He's worried about your safety. You can't defend yourself very well, you know." She grinned at him as he sent a glare her way.

"I know that, Naomi. I really do know that. I just don't want to put anyone in danger." He stared at her again as she began to laugh.

"Nollan? Did you miss something along the way? Richard has a security team. You know? Those people who put themselves in danger, between their clients and the bad guys as we call them? That Timothy, Silver, Stephen, and myself are part of his team? That's what we do, Nollan. That's who we are. Richard has some of the best security that you can find."

Nollan slowly nodded, not having realized how serious Naomi was about this. He sighed to himself. *God? What do I do? Do I stay at home, fumble around to take care of myself, and put myself and my neighbours in danger from someone unknown? Or do*

I take Richard up on his offer to help, to protect me? You have to guide in this, dear Lord. I read the verses on protection, on friends, on Your great love for me. I want to get to know this lady as a friend. It just seems too hard at this point. Nollan waited, knowing that God would answer and that he would have peace about his decision.

Naomi pulled to a stop in Nollan's driveway. He lived just inside the city limits, his house sheltered by towering oak and maple trees with the odd pine tree sprinkled here and there. His home was an old two-story house that Naomi suspected had been built by someone years ago who had money. She liked it. The gingerbread trim was something that she had always wanted on her own home, but a bungalow didn't really suit it.

Turning to Nollan, she found him watching her, a look on his face that said that she was special to him. Her own heart began to loosen from the tight bonds that she had always had in place.

"Nollan? This is nice. I like your home. The landscaping is beautiful." Naomi was out of the truck, her eyes on the move as she searched the area. She didn't have that feeling of being watched but she was too experienced not to know that it would happen at some point.

Chapter 11

Naomi roamed the outside of Nollan's house, searching for anything that should not be there. She was impressed with the security that he had in place. It was as good as Richard, she thought. Whoever had set it up was good. A thought crossed her mind before she shook it off.

Hearing a vehicle, she turned, finding Richard walking towards her. His own eyes were searching before he too nodded. He didn't like all the trees. If they had to make a stand here, Richard knew that it would be difficult but doable.

Naomi walked towards him, a question on her lips that died. Richard would speak when he was ready. Until he did, he would spend that time in prayer. Naomi knew him too well to think otherwise.

"Naomi? Have you looked at his security system?" Richard walked around the house, pausing in the backyard.

"I have, Richard. It's about as good as yours."

"I talked to Abe last night. He had called about Nollan. Word reached him about what had happened. He said that Joseph had set up the system."

"That's why it's so good, then." Naomi turned to face the house, finding Nollan standing nearby. "Nollan?"

"I'm sorry. I wasn't meaning to eavesdrop on your conversation. You know Abe? Of course, you do.” Nollan rubbed at his face. He had managed to shower, shave, and change his clothes, as difficult as it had been. “What now, Richard?”

“Let’s find some seats, Nollan. You’re barely staying upright.” Richard’s hand was out to catch Nollan’s good arm, turning him and directing him to a seat. “We need to talk, Nollan.”

“I know that we do. I get that. I just don’t want to leave my home.” Nollan was adamant about that.

“We know that, Nollan. Everyone that we have ever protected has said the same. But for the next few days, given that you’re handicapped, I would ask that you come and stay with me. It’s your decision.” Richard waited patiently, letting Nollan have the time he required to make that decision

Naomi just prayed for her friend. Somehow, she knew that he would decide to stay at home. And for that, she could not blame him. She would feel the same way. Naomi had had a long discussion with her parents that afternoon, their weekly phone call taking longer than it usually did. Her father had prayed for her, prayed for Nollan, and prayed for her team. He had spoken with Richard when he had been around. He knew what Naomi was likely facing. That worried him but he had no idea what to do about it.

Nollan raised his head at last, searching Richard’s face and then turning to Naomi, his eyes lingering on her. He knew the decision that they wanted him to make. He just couldn’t do that. He had to be in his own home. It was his refuge, his sanctuary,

—

and his place to rest and restore himself. He shook his head at last.

"I think that I'll stay here, Richard. I need access to what I have here in my office. I also need to be able to reach my office. I can do that best from here." Nollan didn't break his contact with Naomi, a frown now on her face.

"We understand that, Nollan. We wanted to make that offer to you. You can expect one or more of us to check in with you more than once in a day. Bill and Lily will also be around. They have many questions for you."

"I understand that as well, Richard. Bill has been in touch. We'll talk tomorrow. As for now, you two have had a long day. You need to get on the road and get home." Nollan rose, said good night, and then walked into his house, the lock clicking closed behind him.

Richard and Naomi shared a look before they were on their feet. Naomi thanked Richard for the lift back to the hospital to claim her car. She drove away, not seeing Richard trailing after her. He was concerned about her, knowing that events would draw her more and more into Nollan's life. And at the moment, no one knew for sure which one of them was being tracked and put in danger.

Naomi curled up on her couch, a blanket covering her. It was still warm out but she felt chilled. She had muted her phone for the time being, just needing the quiet. Her thoughts turned to Nollan, wanting to call him just to reassure herself that he was doing fine. She just refused to do that. It was not her place to do that, she thought.

Her thoughts turned to the events that had happened. She reached for a pen and paper, making her notes, asking her questions, and then summarizing what she had concluded. She set it aside at last, reaching instead for her Bible. She needed that.

Nollan settled down on his bed, pillows positioned to prop up the shoulder and arm. He was in pain, taking the medications that would ease it but also make him sleep. He didn't want to do that but it was necessary. His thoughts turned to the questions that Bill had asked him. He would make the lists that Bill asked for, putting down anyone and everyone that he could think of. Nollan knew that there were certain names that he could not in good conscience give him.

Bill was frustrated. He had spoken with both Naomi and Nollan, not reaching a good conclusion. He didn't have enough facts to do that. Not yet, at any rate. He would need to set it aside at some point, he knew, unless something else happened. And that it would, that was a certainty.

Lily approached his office, a folder in her hand. She silently set it down and walked away. She too was troubled about her friend and decided that she would head Naomi's way later on. That had been her plan until a call came in about a murder and she had to head that way. She didn't want to but it was her work and it was calling her.

Andrew rose at last from his desk, his paperwork done for the night. He was heading home but walked through the department, speaking with each officer, standing at last in Bill's office doorway. Bill looked up, shaking his head at the question on Andrew's face. Both men sighed. They wanted it over for Naomi but knew that it would take time.

Richard paused as he stood in his front doorway before heading for his favourite seat on the front porch. His mug of coffee hit the railing before he sat, his head bowing as he prayed for his friends. He considered Nollan a friend now. He had observed the looks that Nollan and Naomi were shooting towards each other. He smiled to himself. Nollan seemed to be just right for Naomi. His head bent as he prayed for his friends, knowing that it was just going to get worse for them before it got better.

Chapter 12

Three days later, Nollan stared at himself in the bathroom mirror. He could see the lines of pain that were etched into his face. He was still in pain, almost as bad as it had been. He was taking the medications but didn't find them effective. He was due to see the surgeon in a couple of days. Perhaps at that point, he would have more answers on how he was healing.

He turned as he heard his phone, heading for his office to retrieve it. He swiped it open, seeing that he had missed a call from his aunt. Calling her back at the moment was not an option. He instead sent off a quick text to her.

Walking through his office building, Nollan paused as he stood in his workroom. He still had nightmares about his attack. He had sought counsel with his pastor, Silas. Silas had shared the adventure, as they termed it, that he and his wife, Madigan, had gone through. Nollan had not expected it.

Hearing footsteps, Nollan froze for a moment before he cautiously walked towards the front of the building. He blew out the breath that he had been holding.

"Timothy? What are you doing here?" Nollan was puzzled.

"Nollan? And how are you today?" Timothy grinned at him. "About like that?" Timothy knew to a certain extent how Nollan would be feeling. "I'm here with you today. Richard has decided that you need protection.”

“I do? Has something happened to Naomi?” He was more worried about his friend than himself.

“Naomi is with the others. She’s safe. You, on the other hand, are not. Someone needs to be with you today.”

Nollan stared at him, shook his head, and walked back to his workroom. He had investigations on the go, searching for an answer for a small healthcare company. Timothy walked through the building, stopping to speak with the secretary, and then heading for Nollan. He leaned a shoulder against the doorframe, watching Nollan. He knew that it would be a long day but that was how it worked in his business.

Nollan stepped back at the end of the day. He had been successful in what he needed to accomplish. The company’s CEO had been grateful for his call. He stretched as best he could, yawned, and then turned to head for his office. He squinted at the clock as he did so. It was late, after five o’clock. Timothy’s appearance in front of him startled him.

“I thought that you had left. I didn’t hear you all day.” Nollan reached for his briefcase, intent on heading for home. “I’ll lock up after you, Timothy. You need to get home to your wife.”

“And I will. I’ll trail you home and then walk through it.” Timothy simply stared back at Nollan.

Nollan nodded, knowing that nothing he could say would sway Timothy from that. Richard’s team was moving in and taking care of him. He knew that it was for himself but he was also wise enough to realize that part of it was for Naomi. He smiled to himself as he drove through town. He had plans for that weekend. He just prayed that Naomi would be free and agreeable to spending some time with him.

Timothy headed for his car, heading for him. He had sent off a quick text to Richard, letting him know that all was well.

Naomi turned from her door that evening. She had been hoping that it might be Nollan. Instead, it was Lily.

"Lily? Are you on duty?" Naomi headed for the kitchen, her eyes on the clock. She was hungry and had just been about to make her supper.

"Nope. I'm off tonight. I'm here to spend some time with a friend, if that friend wants." Lily grinned at her friend.

"This friend wants. Have you eaten?" Naomi turned as Lily laughed, holding up a pizza box.

"I know that you were likely just getting home. I took a chance on our favourite pie." Lily dropped the pizza box to the countertop before reaching for some plates.

"I haven't. That sounds good. How long can you stay?" Naomi needed a friend to talk to. Lily was the perfect one to do that with.

"How are you really doing, Naomi?" Lily continued dishing out the pizza, setting the plates on the table as Naomi reached into the fridge for bottles of water.

Naomi shrugged, not sure how to respond. She knew that Lily was concerned, not just as a police officer, but also as a friend. Her prayer on an hourly basis was for Nollan and his protection. She knew from experience that it was only God who could do that. They could be as experienced and equipped as well as they could be. Yet, things still went wrong.

"I'm not sure any more, Lily. My body is healing. My mind is slowing down some and healing. The emotions are back in control. I just worry." She reached for her piece of pizza and bit into it.

"I know what you aren't saying, Naomi." Lily wiped her mouth with the paper napkin. Her thoughts turned to the blessing that Naomi had prayed over their food. She heard the silent, unspoken plea in her words. "You're hurting for Nollan."

"I am. I don't know which of us was the target. My team has gone over everything that we can for the fourth time." She blew out a breath, knowing that there was nothing there. "I didn't see anything there. None of us did. So, what happened? How did I connect with Nollan?"

"That's what we're looking at. We're looking into both of your backgrounds, just as you know that we would. Nollan's background so far is interesting."

"I know that it is. He's chosen an interesting career path. There could be something there but that doesn't explain why the bomb was placed on my car. It takes time to do that."

"And it was possible. You and he took time to eat your meal. Then you headed through the kitchen, stopping there to talk. That would have given someone with experience in this to set it. The man who approached you? We still don't have confirmation of his name. People are afraid to talk about him."

"I know. I have asked Emma to look into it. She's been tied up in some urgent investigations that have taken her time and her staff's time. She thought that by today she could free someone to start a search. I'm scared, Lily. And you know that I don't scare easily."

Lily nodded, knowing how fearless Naomi was. The whole team was like that.

"I know, Naomi. I know that. God will protect you. You just might not like what you have to go through. Not one of our friends did."

"No, they didn't. I need to talk to them."

"You do and you will. For tonight, we set it aside." Lily was on her feet, helping to clear the table and set the remaining portion of the pizza in the fridge. "Now what?"

"Now what? One of our favourite movies is on. Do you have time for it?"

"I do. I'm on the late shift tomorrow. Let's watch it and then I can head for home."

Laughter at the funny scenes and tears at the sad scenes in the movie was the order of their evening. Once Lily had walked away, Naomi walked the perimeter of her home and yard, the light from the flashlight flickering in the darkness. She headed inside, locking up after herself. Naomi reached for her phone, knowing that she was likely swamped with messages. That always happened with her phone was on mute.

Naomi smiled at the messages from the men on her team. Her finger lingered as she pulled up the message from Nollan, a smile appearing on her face. He was special, she decided, looking out for her even now. Her thoughts turned to prayer, asking for protection for her friend. He had been injured, twice. She just asked that it not happen again, but she had to add in her prayer that it had to be at God's will.

Chapter 13

Two weeks later, Nollan walked through his town, his eyes watchful. He knew that he was being followed. He had noticed the shadows behind him and the vehicles trailing him around town. There was evidence that they ha bd been around his home and office building. They just had not been able to get in. Of that, Nollan was thankful.

Today, he had been determined to set it all aside. His hand had Naomi's tight in his. He had approached her the night before, asking what her plans were for Saturday, the next day. She had snorted, causing him to laugh.

"I don't have plans." She had told him. "No plans. Except for staying home and vegetating."

"Vegetating, huh? Would you spend it with me? I would like to, if you would allow me that." Nollan had almost held his breath.

"That would be nice, Nollan. Thank you for asking. What time do you want me to meet you?"

"I'm picking you up. I'm back driving."

Nollan had been as good as his word. He arrived mid-morning, finding Naomi waiting for him. He had grinned at her, reached for her hand, and tucked her into his truck.

"Where to, Naomi?"

"I don't know. Where were you planning on spending the day?"

"In my town. Is that okay?" Nollan waited for Naomi to respond. He would not force her to do that. If she refused, then they would find a compromise.

"I would like that. I like your town. And I suspect that there will be a high tea waiting at your aunt's?"

"I would like that, if you agree." He had grinned again as she nodded.

Naomi studied the man with her. *He's tall,* she thought, *just like all the other men in my life. Lord, protect us this day. We need to have some fun but I am afraid. It is only You who knows the framework that we live in. Thank You for that. And as Richard says, I love you.*

Nollan pointed to a nearby shop, leading Naomi that way. Her mouth opened for a moment as she stared around, entranced with the artwork that was there.

"I didn't know this was here. I would have been in here before." Naomi looked up at him, her face alight.

"It's been here for years. Angel is a high-school friend. She works closely with someone in Elmton as well just to showcase artists' work." He pointed to the sun catchers. "These are my favourites."

Naomi moved that way, a hand out to gently touch one of them.

"These are beautiful. Whoever the artist is, they're very talented."

"It's a lady from your town. She has her own stained-glass shop." Nollan started to move away until Naomi's hand stopped him.

"Faith. She's a friend. No wonder these looked familiar."

"You know her?" Nollan had wanted to meet the artist. He just didn't know who she was.

"She is. I'll introduce you to her and her husband. They go to our church. In fact, they had an adventure. We have had quite a few friends who have."

"Is that a fact?" Nollan grinned at her before reaching for the sun catcher that had caught Naomi's attention. She gave him a querying look before she walked around the room. She didn't see Nollan trailing her, reaching once in a while for something that she had lingered over. He headed for the cash desk, paying for them and then heading quickly for his truck to tuck them into the cab.

Naomi watched for him, seeing him walking back through the store. She frowned for a moment, seeing someone following him before they walked past the store.

"Hungry, my love?" Nollan grinned at her.

"I am. Your aunt's expecting you, isn't she?" She grinned at him in return.

"She is. Thank you for today, Naomi. I have enjoyed it so much. Now, I have one more store to show you before we head for the tea room."

Naomi looked in askance at him once more as he led her into a florist. He greeted the sales clerk before he turned to her.

"What are your favourite flowers?" He continued to grin at her as her mouth dropped open

Naomi snapped her mouth closed. Just what was he up to, she wondered.

"Nollan? My favourite flower?"

"Yes. Your favourite flowers. I need to buy some flowers for a beautiful lady who has spent the day with me." He continued to grin at her, nodding at the sales clerk as she waited.

"I would say carnations and daisies." She frowned at him as he turned her towards the cooler in the store.

"Sally. You heard the lady. Carnations and daisies for the lady."

Naomi took the bouquet, a blush on her face. She was not used to receiving flowers, at least not from a man.

"Thank you, Nollan. This is so sweet." Naomi's face was raised to him, a happy look on it. She stilled as Nollan dropped a kiss on her cheek and then led her away.

Nollan stopped by the truck, leaving her bouquet safe, before they headed for Maggie's tea room. Seated at her favourite table, Naomi watched him closely. Catching movement, Naomi's gaze raised, a frown on her face. She didn't or couldn't pinpoint who had moved but someone had. She drew in a deep breath. Of course, something like that would happen. Someone had been following them, of that she was certain.

Nollan had his eyes on his lady, as he had become to think of her. He could tell that she had gone into work mode and that disturbed him. He had wanted to spend some fun time with her. Only, it didn't seem to be working out that way.

Chapter 14

Driving home that night, Nollan yawned. It had been a long day, he decided, but an enjoyable one. He had dropped Naomi off at her home, walking her to her door. He had hugged her and walked away, the bag with the items that he had purchased set on the table in her entryway. He smiled. She had such a dry sense of humour, he decided.

Slamming on the brakes, Nollan reached for the lock button on his door, ensuring that his doors were locked. The car in front of him had come to a sudden spot, the tail lights gleaming red in the dusk. There was no way that he was getting out. He reached for his phone, simply calling for help. He told the dispatcher that he had no idea what was going on but that he didn't feel safe.

A man approached each side of his truck, pounding at the windows to make him take them down. He refused, knowing that he shouldn't. It would not be to his benefit to do so. The emergency lights that lit up the night sky startled the two men, who turned and ran. The car was abandoned in front of him.

The officer spoke with Nollan, taking his statement before he headed for the car. He searched it, finding rope and a loaded syringe. He turned to stare back at Nollan who was staring back at him.

"Bill?" Lily came looking for him. Both detectives were working late that night. "A patrol officer just called in. He is with Nollan. It appears that someone was trying to abduct him tonight."

"What?" Bill was on his feet. "Where?"

"Near his home. He says that two men approached Nollan's truck and then took off when they saw the patrol vehicle. They ditched their vehicle there."

"And it will be stolen, no doubt. Okay. Head that way. Keep me in the loop. I have to work through this statement. If you need me, I'll spring myself free and head that way." Bill paused, a thoughtful look on his face. "Naomi?"

"He was alone. He told the officer that they had spent the day away and that he was coming from dropping her at her home. This is bizarre. I can't get a handle on who or why."

"None of us can. We need to sit down with Nollan again next week. It seems to be directed at him."

"It does. But that could be to throw us off. You do know that?" Lily grinned at him before she sobered. "I worry about Naomi, Bill. She's vulnerable whether she will admit it or not."

"She is. She's quite capable of taking care of herself. Unfortunately, so were her team mates and look what happened to them." Bill watched Lily walk away before he sat down again, working through his paperwork. He paused at one point, his head raising at a thought. Nodding, he reached for his phone.

"Richard? What on your books for Monday?" Bill had no hesitation in asking that.

—

"Monday? It's paperwork day. We don't have a team in but we're needing to get caught up. It shouldn't take that long." Richard paused before he nodded. "You want to meet with the team."

"We need to. This is getting worse for Naomi. I need to reach out to your team to get your thoughts on what we can put in plans for both her and Nollan."

Richard set his phone on the side table, his thoughts troubled. He had no idea what Naomi had become involved in, but it had to be bad for Bill to request a meeting such as he had. He reached for his phone again, simply sending out a text to all of his team that they were meeting with Bill on Monday. Any thoughts, ideas, or plans would be greatly appreciated.

Naomi frowned at the message and then sighed. She felt as if her freedom was getting up and running, not walking, away from her. And that likely meant the same for Nollan. She did not want to go into protective custody. Not yet, anyway. That likely meant that Nollan's had as well.

Timothy reached to hug his wife. Tate had been a blessing sent to him from God, he always told her. He worried about her but not as much as he had.

"What's wrong, love?" Tate leaned back in his arms, studying the worry on his face.

"Richard wants a meeting on Monday with Bill. That doesn't sound good. Something has to have happened to do that."

"I'm sure that there has been. Naomi is due for lunch tomorrow. I asked Nollan as well. He was glad to accept when he found on Naomi would be here. Are they a couple or something?” She grinned at him.

Timothy began to laugh. Tate had asked the question that Naomi’s friends were dancing around.

“I would say a couple. I heard that they spent the day in his town.” Timothy reached for the plate of food that Tate was handing him.

“They did?” Tate thought about that after Timothy had asked the blessing on their food. “I can see that. They seem to suit one another.”

“They do. I need to speak with Mae and see what she’s heard.” Mae, a neighbour across the street, was a retired officer. “She still has her ear to the pulse of this town.”

“She always will, Timothy. We both know that.” Tate continued to eat even as her thoughts stayed with her friend. She decided that the four ladies of the team needed to meet. Even though two were spouses, they were still part of the team. There was not a doubt about that.

Naomi walked through her house late that night. Nollan had called, just to ask if he could pick her up for church in the morning. She had happily agreed. There had been something off about him though. She was determined that she would find out in the morning.

Stopping in the entryway, Naomi stared through the door window before she turned with a sigh. She was missing her family. She needed to make a trip that way and soon. Her eyes stopped on the bag sitting on the table. Naomi didn’t remember setting it there. She was cautious in touching it, feeling it. The odds shapes concerned her.

Reaching into the bag, Naomi pulled out tissue-wrapped items. She began to unwrap them, stopping as she stared and studied each one. Nollan, she thought. He bought everything that I hesitated at without buying. Her face grew soft as she lifted up a glass angel. Her guardian angel, she decided. She hunted for her phone, sending off a quick thank you.

Nollan had been waiting for that. He had retired but was not yet asleep. His thoughts had gone back over the day, ending with the situation that he had faced on the drive home. Lily had been forthright with him. They didn't know who it was. Could he explain?

Shaking his head, Nollan had not been able to. He set it aside for the night, knowing that he would be speaking with Naomi in the morning. A smile grew across his face as he read her thank you. He simply replied with a heart icon.

Chapter 15

Naomi watched as Nollan walked back towards her as she waited outside the church building the next morning. She could see that he was tired, his steps showing that. He looked up at her and smiled, his hand reaching for hers.

"How's the healing?" Nollan looked around at the question, seeing Stephen and Shanli hear them.

"They're healing. The pain is much better. I see the surgeon this week. Hopefully, I can ditch the sling."

Stephen began to laugh. He knew what he would have felt like if it had been him.

"I agree with you. Come on. Let's find our seats. I have really been enjoying Silas' messages on protection."

"So have I. They have been so apt." Nollan waited for Naomi to sit before he sat beside her. "I hear that you're invited to Timothy's for lunch." He had a small smile on his face as he waited for her to respond.

"I am. And you are too, aren't you?" Naomi smirked at him.

"I am. Thank you, Naomi, for being who you are."

Mid-afternoon, Timothy pointed towards his office, Nollan following as he walked that way. Nollan roamed the room, nodding.

—

"I like your office, Timothy. It's comfortable but a place where you can work."

"It is. I wanted that. Tate has put her touch in here as well." Timothy pointed to a chair. "I have a burden for you, Nollan. What can you tell me? And if you do say anything, do I have your permission to pass it on to the team?"

Nollan nodded, knowing that was what had to happen.

"I agree, Timothy. That needs to be done. I'm worried about Naomi." He waved his hand as Timothy began to laugh. "I know. She can take care of herself. I still worry. I don't know if it's because of me or her."

"We all understand that, Nollan. We're worried about her too. She's very independent. Now, if you're looking for somewhere to hide, Naomi would be able to find that. She's the one on the team who sources our safe houses."

"I see." Nollan waited, not sure how to phrase his question. "You each have a specialty?"

"We do. I look after our vehicles. Stephen is our paramedic. Silver is our investigator. Naomi, as I said, is the one who finds our safe houses. Richard is our coordinator of everything."

Nollan's eyes were on Timothy as he spoke. He nodded, one of his questions answered.

"If someone wanted to go after Richard, how would they do that?"

Timothy nodded once more. Nollan was asking the questions that they were.

"By going after each one of us. And we know that has happened with three of us. There were things that were not explained, couldn't be explained. I suspect the same with happen with Naomi. But for you? Explain to me what you do."

Nollan did just that, Timothy reaching to make notes.

"So if someone wanted to sabotage something, they could? But that's why you research. You've turned more to investigations, haven't you?"

"I have. I have always liked a mystery. This fits me well." Nollan grew quiet, his thoughts on his parents. "Mom and Dad supported me in my goal. I lost them in an accident when I was just starting college. Aunt Maggie took me in. She's my Mom's sister. She and Uncle Jake supported me too."

"Tell me then. Who would know what you are working on? What you are researching and investigating?"

"No one. I mean my secretary sees some of it, but I do all the reports myself and send them off myself. She would know the company but not the request." Nollan's brow wrinkled as he thought it through. "I can't think of anyone other than myself and the person who asked me. I have high security on my computer. The passwords are as secure as I can make them and I change them regularly."

"Okay. It's not from your end. So it has to be someone with one of the companies. Is there an investigation that stands out to you?"

Nollan shook his head.

"I can't think of one. Bill asked me to go back over everything." Nollan looked up as the ladies approached, his hand reached for Naomi's, pulling herself down beside him, not seeing the look that Timothy and Tate shared.

Bill walked back from the downtown area of town. He was worn out already and the week was just starting. Another violent crime that didn't need to happen had called him out on a Sunday. He slipped into his chair, dropping his notepad in front of him. Reaching for his keyboard, Bill worked away on his notes, looking up as he heard a knock at his door.

"Abe? You're here?" Bill reached to shake Abe Finlay's hand. "What brings you to town?"

"Naomi does. Emma has spoken with her and is very concerned about her." Abe sat, handing Bill an envelope. "This is what she has found already. I don't like it."

"What is it that you don't like?"

"You are friends with Naomi. You know her family. What none of us knew is that her grandfather was murdered. That murderer was released from prison this year. He was a young man at the time. He'd been in his fifties now, I think Emma said. For some reason, he blames Naomi. We haven't been able to determine why. Emma's still investigating that but she's not getting too far. Likely because most of the people that she needs to reach out to are deceased. She's pulled the reports, talked to whomever she can, and collated it for you. I hope that it helps. Someone needs to talk to Naomi and her family."

"And that would be me. I'm meeting with Richard's team tomorrow. I'll make sure that I talk to her. I'll reach out to her parents tomorrow morning." Bill yawned, causing Abe to laugh. "Sorry, it's been a long day already. Just too many cases."

"There always are. Call Emma if you need to. She's expecting it." Abe walked away, leaving Bill staring down at the folder before he opened it and began to read.

Chapter 16

A hand covering her mouth, Naomi stared at Bill the next afternoon. It was not possible, she decided, that a grandfather had been murdered. Her parents would have told her she was certain.

"You're serious, aren't you, Bill?" Naomi paced away from him.

Bill watched her, his eyes compassionate. He had not realized that this would be news to her.

"You didn't know?"

Bill's voice reached through the fog that she was that she was fighting her way through. She turned back to him, not seeing her team members watching her closely as they gathered in the room.

"No, I didn't. I mean, Mom and Dad just said that he died suddenly. I need to talk to them."

"Later, Naomi. For now, we need to concentrate on someone else. We'll come back to that. Are you able to do that?"

Naomi shook her head, walking away, leaving everyone staring after her.

"Let her have some time, Bill. She'll be reaching out to her parents. We'll let her have that. She'll be back." Richard reached for the folder on the table. "We'll work through this. If Naomi's not back by the time that we're done, one of us will find her."

Naomi walked away from the office, heading for her car. She was leaving and heading home. Richard would have expected that, she knew.

Reaching her home, she almost ran for the office. Pulling up an investigative website that they used, she searched for her grandfather's name, sitting back in horror as she read the reports. She reached to print them, gathering them up, knowing that Richard and her friends would need them.

Her phone rang at that point. She swiped the screen, seeing that it was her mother. She wasn't ready to speak with her yet but she had to.

"Mom? You're calling during the day."

"I am, dear. Dad and I are almost at your place. Your sisters are with us. We need to talk." Her mother's voice sounded as if she had been weeping.

"About Grandpa?" Naomi heard the silence at the other end of the phone.

"Yes. But how did you know?"

"Bill. He's somehow found out about it. I did some research, Mom. We do need to talk."

Naomi was on her feet, heading for the kitchen, knowing that she would need to have a meal ready for them. She reached for the freezer, pulling out a couple of casseroles and shoving them into the oven.

Benjamin hugged his daughter, hoping on just a bit longer than he usually did. Her sisters and mother had hugged her and then walked into the house, a quietness about them that was unusual.

"Dad? Is it true?"

"That my Dad was murdered? Yes. I'm sorry that we never told you. We were estranged at the time. He didn't want anything to do with us. At that point, you were all so small that we didn't tell you. And it just got easier not to say anything."

"And as time went by, it just became so much harder to do so. I get that, Dad. Now we need to." Naomi headed for where she could hear her mother and sisters.

Benjamin's head dropped for a moment. He and Eve had never wanted to do this. Now, they needed to whether they wanted to or not. He looked up as he heard Nora's voice, calling him to come for his supper.

Naomi helped clear off the table, quiet conversation between Nora, Nikki, and their mother. She was disturbed, to say the least. She had to walk away from her family for a moment, heading for her office. She reached for her phone, checking her messages.

Richard's message stopped her, causing her to raise her head to stare at the doorway. She simply replied to him that she was okay, that her family was here, and that they would talk in the morning. She would be there as usual.

Nollan's message had her staring at it, not sure what he was saying. He had texted that he was worried about her and that he was praying for her. Did she need him to come over or anything? He would do that for her. He followed that statement with a heart. Her face softened as she re-read it. She sent him a text as well just to let him know that she was okay. She would talk with him later. Would he grant her that? And she thanked him for his prayers.

Eve had come looking for her youngest daughter, waiting in the hallway as she saw that Naomi was on her phone. As Naomi set it aside, Eve walked towards her, wrapping her into a mom hug. Naomi clung to her mother, somehow knowing that the conversation to come would change their lives

"Naomi, come. We're wanting to spend some time in prayer. Then, we'll talk. If it's all right with you, we'll spend the night. That way, we can talk as long as we need to." Eve was hesitant to do that, even though Naomi had always welcomed them into her home.

"It's okay, Mom. It's okay. I have the reports that we need, I think. I can understand why you didn't tell us. It just leaves questions."

"We know it does. But your grandfather refused to have anything to do with us. That started just before your Dad and I married. We could never understand it." Eve's arm around her daughter turned her towards the door.

"What about Grandma? She never said anything." Naomi had spent time thinking back over the family.

"She never talked about him. She did tell me on one occasion that she was ashamed to have been married to him. When he was killed, he was under investigation for criminal activities. We were never sure or were never told if he really had been."

"I have that information, Mom. A friend researched him and sent me information. She is still working on it. She can find reports that no one else can."

"That's good. Let her know that we'll pay for her time." Benjamin just stared at his daughter as she shook her head. "Is that a problem?"

"She won't take a penny, Dad. She never does with friends. She'll keep looking into it and then forward everything that she can find. And she will find information that others think is not findable."

Benjamin nodded, not doubting her words but still not sure that would happen.

Chapter 17

Richard found Naomi in her office when he walked into the building the next day. He frowned. She was in early, he knew. He simply sat in a chair in front of her desk and waited, praying for her as he did so.

Naomi glanced up for a moment, her eyes meeting Richard's before they dropped. She hesitated and then handed over the folder she had just closed. He took it, a question on his face

"It's about my family, Richard. I don't know if you had this information or not. If you want me to leave the team, then I will. This may impact how our team works."

"I doubt that, Naomi. Give me the condensed version of this." Richard waited patiently.

"The condensed version? Mom and Dad never said anything. He just said that we were so young when it happened that they didn't tell us. Mom said that Grandma didn't say much either, only was ashamed. The long story short? Grandpa had lost most of his savings. In order to recover, he took to fraud and blackmail. One of the families that he was blackmailing had a son in his twenties. He found out, confronted Grandpa, and shot him. He took a plea bargain. His time is served, so he is out. They're not sure if he has come after one of us or not. He has disappeared from their area even though he isn't supposed to leave that area. They're trying to track him but haven't found him."

———

"How old would he be now?" Richard flipped through the paperwork, stopping at the photo that Naomi had included.

"In his early fifties or late forties. I haven't been able to find an exact birthdate for him. Nor has Emma. It keeps changing for some reason, even in all the legal paperwork."

"It does? Naomi, I am about to ask you a question. I want you to think about your answer." He handed over the photo, his eyes on her.

She reached for it, her eyes returning his stare.

"Richard? What are you asking?"

"I am asking if you know this man."

Naomi nodded before her eyes dropped to the photo. She drew in a deep breath. She knew him.

"That's the man who said that he had a team that he wanted us to train. He doesn't, does he? Silver wasn't finding any information on him."

"And she won't. He gave us an alias. This needs to get to Bill and Lily. You also need to alert Nollan." Richard's head tilted as he watched her face. "Naomi?"

"He's the one who was in the tea room that day. That was my fault?" Naomi was horrified.

"We don't know that you are. We'll have Emma continue to search for him. Bill will as well. He's got to be working with someone. If he has just been released from prison, he not like will have a lot of resources available. It looks as if his parents are deceased. And his family doesn't want anything to do with him. At least not on paper."

"That's what I was picking up." Naomi looked towards her office door where the other three team members had gathered. "Listen, guys. We've identified the man from the tea room. Richard has that information. Apparently, he killed my paternal grandfather. I'm sorry. I just found this out last night."

"That's not your fault, Naomi." Stephen reached for the photo. "He's been hanging around town. I've seen him more than once." He tilted his hand to show Silver and Stephen the photo.

"He has been. I've seen him around here as well. In fact, he was on the property last week. He's the one that we asked to leave." Timothy looked towards Richard, finding him nodding.

"That's correct. Now, you who are on training duty, head off. Naomi, you're not. We're heading to find Bill and Lily. Then, we find your fellow and warn him."

Naomi finally remembered to snap her mouth closed. Just what had Richard meant? She sighed. She knew what he meant. *Lord, I do treasure Nollan's friendship. And I am scared for him and for myself. Protect us, Lord.*

Richard nodded to himself. Naomi was thinking hard, he knew.

"Listen, Naomi. I don't need to give you my talk. The one that you're always teasing me about. You've heard it so many times that you could give it.

———

94

You know that God has you in the hollow of His hand. He doesn't want anything else but the best for you. You also know that He allows events to happen in our lives that we would just as soon avoid. It's part of His plan for your lives. You know the verses from scripture that I pull out. Study them. Give them to Nollan. And yes, he's your guy. We can all see that." Richard was on his feet, folder in his head, striding from the building.

Naomi grabbed what she needed to and ran after him. Seated in his car, she thought through what he had said. She knew that he was correct. God never left them, not for one moment.

"Thank you, Richard. I needed that reminder." Naomi stared at the photo, memorizing what she could. "How do we find him?"

"Bill will circulate the photo. The people on the street will be looking for him. They'll find him. We know how they work."

"We do. We've seen it so many times. Look how Old George and Jason helped."

"They did at that. We will do what we can to keep you and Nollan safe." Richard parked in front of the police department, turning off the ignition, and then shifting to watch Naomi. "You said that your family came through last night?"

"They did. They were here until early this morning before they headed home. We needed that time together. Dad said that he would continue to look for information if he could. I just don't know if he'll find anything. I'm afraid for him, Richard, if he does that."

"I get that, Naomi. I'll speak with him if you like." Richard watched as she finally nodded. "Now, how be we take that information in to Bill and see what he has to say?" Richard saw Bill waiting for them.

"I guess. I don't know if it will help." Naomi opened the door, finding Bill waiting for her to come towards him.

"Naomi? What did you go and do?" Bill asked that half in a jesting manner.

Naomi held up the folder.

"This, Bill. The man who was in the tea room that day? I just discovered that he killed my paternal grandfather. Isn't that enough?" Tears momentarily blinded her, causing Bill and Richard to share a glance. She did not cry, they knew.

Chapter 18

Bill flipped through the folder, reading the information. He stopped on the photo and studied it. He knew the man as well. He had been around town for the last month or so. Bill also knew that the man had been identified as a suspect in many break and enters. He just couldn't understand how word was out that this man was an assassin. It didn't make sense if he was in prison.

"Naomi, did you come up with a brother or a twin or some family member who looked like this man?" Bill looked up as she didn't speak.

Naomi shook her head.

"I haven't. Emma hasn't said." Her phone was out. "Let me send Mom or Dad a text. They would be able to tell me." She waited, knowing that one of her parents would be back to her as soon as they could. She nodded as her father responded. "He has a brother, a year younger than him, Dad thinks. He's in and out of our town all the time. Dad has no idea what he does for a living." She looked up at Bill. "Is he the one who's the assassin?"

Bill had been searching for the man once he had the name, nodding at last.

"He could be. They do look alike." He rose as he printed off the man's photo. He had a prayer in his heart as he handed the photo to Naomi. "Take a look at this man, Naomi. I know that you feel the murderer is the one who you feel was in the tea room. Confirm for me if it is possible that it was this man?"

Naomi took the picture and stared at it. Fear rose in her as she studied it, feeling the evil coming from the man even through the photo.

"No, it was the other man. This man? I've seen him around. Not in the last week or so." She almost threw the photo back at Bill. She then wrapped her arms around herself. "We need to warn Nollan."

"And we will. I'll talk with him today." Bill rose as Richard Naomi walked away. He headed for Andrew, spoke with him briefly, and then headed for Lily.

"Lily? Where are you in the investigation involving Naomi?"

"Not where I want to be. What do you have there?" Lily pointed at the folder in his hand.

"This? Naomi's been busy as had Emma. They've provided a photo of and identified the man in the tea room. They have also identified the assassin that we've been hearing about."

"They have?" Lily reached for the folder, then was on her feet, copying the material and handing the originals back to Bill. "You want me working on this?"

"I do, for at least today. Reach out to Emma and talk with her. Check with your sources on the streets. You know the drill just as well as I do. I spoke with Andrew. He's aware of what has been provided." Bill walked away, dropping the folder on his desk. He

—

opened it to the photos, snapping copies of them, and then shut the folder. He then headed for his car, knowing that he would have to interrupt Nollan whether that man was willing to let him do that or not.

Nollan looked around as he heard Bill's voice. He stared down at the paperwork that he had just finished before he rubbed at his collarbone. It was sore that he had to admit. It was healing well, he had been told.

Bill looked around from where he was standing at a window, studying Nollan. This was taking a toll on him, Bill decided. They needed to end it. Only they couldn't.

"Bill? You're here again? What can I do for you?" Nollan was not backing down this time.

"We need to talk, Nollan. Your lady brought in some information for me. I have some photos that I need you to look at."

Nollan sighed to himself. So much for getting away. He pointed towards his office.

"Have a seat in there. I just need to leave this on the desk. I'll be right in."

Nollan hesitated in the hallway, his thoughts turning to Naomi. *What have you gone and done, love? What did you give Bill that sent him this way? Lord, protect my lady.*

"Nollan. I need to show you two photos. Take a good look at them. Tell me if you recognize either one of the men. Then, we'll talk."

Bill laid the photos on Nollan's desk, his eyes on the other man. Nollan drew in a deep breath and stared down at them.

"This one. This is, I think, the man at Naomi's car." His finger tapped at the photo of the murderer. "The other man? He looks like him but I don't know him. Who are they?"

"The first man? He is a murderer. Naomi has informed us that he killed her paternal grandfather. This has just come to light." Bill stopped speaking, seeing the horror on Nollan's face and hearing his sharply indrawn breath. "The other man? He's the brother. We don't have all the information on him yet that we want before we say much. Just watch yourself, Nollan. If he's looking for you, he means you harm." Bill walked away at last, warning Nollan as much as he was able to.

Nollan was horrified to say the least. Alone in the building, he paced and prayed, his thoughts on Naomi. He suddenly turned and locked his building, heading for his truck. Once in it, he turned it towards Naomi's, praying that she was safe. He parked and was out of the truck, on the move as quickly as he could. He tugged at the sling, wanting to get rid of it. Only he was not yet able to.

Naomi looked around as she heard the knocking at her door. Almost frenzied knocking, she thought. She walked slowly that way, searching for who it was. Peeking out, she frowned. Nollan? He was here? He looked too worried, she decided.

Pulling open the door, she faced him. Nollan stared at her and then just reached to hug her tightly. He moved her back so that he could close and lock the door before wrapping her into his arms once more. He stood that way for a few moments before she shoved at him. He loosened his arms enough so that she could look up at him.

"Nollan? What is going on?" Naomi loved at him and moved back, pacing away and then back to face him.

"Bill was around. He showed me the photos. How did you find them?"

"The photos? He showed them to you?"

"He did. He said the first man, the man from the tea room, killed your grandfather. He didn't tell me much about the second man. Again, Naomi, what is going on? And would you have even spoken to me about them?" Nollan was angry, not at Naomi, and very much afraid for his lady.

Naomi sighed and silently thanked Bill for leaving it for her to explain. She simply reached for Nollan's hand, drawing him to the kitchen. She delayed the inevitable by making him coffee and herself tea. Setting the mugs down, she sat, her eyes on him.

"We do need to talk, Nollan. But we need to pray more. Will you?" She simply bowed her head as she waited for him to respond.

Chapter 19

Nollan reached for Naomi's hand when he had finished his prayer. He saw the stress and pain on her face, her emotions not kept tightly controlled in his presence any more. Naomi had learned to trust Nollan with her feelings. He was grateful for that. Nollan was falling in love with the beautiful lady sitting near him.

"Naomi? Can you tell me what this is about?"

Naomi nodded, feeling the rush of fear and anger in her. She prayed for that to be removed. She had to let God have those feelings.

"I can. I found out yesterday that my paternal grandfather was involved in fraud and blackmail. He was murdered by the son of one of his victims. He has just been released from prison. He has disappeared, but we know where he is. The other man? That's his brother. He's an assassin from what I understand."

"An assassin? How did he find you?" Nollan was horrified at the thought. "And who is he after?"

"That we don't know. We don't have enough information to determine that. That's where we need to work together and with my team, Emma, and Bill or Lily. Andrew will need to be involved at least on the need to know basis. This is where it is going to get dangerous. We'll need to you work back through your clients. Bill will likely drop a warrant on you to get a list of them. Provide it. It may be the one thing that could solve this. Somehow or other, they have connected us and not just from the tea room."

"That's what I've been trying to work through. How do we do this then, love?"

Nollan didn't catch the term of endearment that slipped out. Naomi didn't miss it, however, a soft smile lighting up her face.

"We start by trying to see where we connect other than with Maggie. Our colleges, churches, trips, interests, clubs, that kind of thing. Friends?"

Nollan nodded, knowing what she was saying.

"I can do that. Listen, I would like to ask you out on a date. A real date. Dinner. A walk." Nollan didn't look at her, afraid that he would see rejection on her face.

Naomi blinked against the tears that suddenly blocked her sight. She simply reached for his hand, causing him to raise his head.

"I would like that, Nollan. Thank you."

Nollan rose at last, taking the copies of the paperwork with him that Naomi had given him. He needed to head home but he didn't want to leave Naomi. He was just so afraid for her.

Naomi walked into work the next morning, finding all the other team members there. She nodded at them, heading for her office for a moment to drop off what she carried. She then went searching for them, finding them gathered in Richard's office.

Richard looked at her, a frown on his face. Something had changed with her overnight, he decided. He just wasn't sure what.

"Richard? You have explained to the others and shown them the photos?" Naomi didn't wait for him to speak.

"I have. They all have copies of the photos as well. Now, let's spend some time in prayer before the training begins. Naomi, we're working through plans for you and Nollan. I want your input on houses." Richard did not wait for her to speak. He knew that she would when she was ready. Instead, he simply led his team in prayer.

Naomi headed for the training building, Stephen at her side. He didn't say anything, just kept watch around them. Silver had watched her walk away before she spoke.

"Richard? What do we do? We have to do something."

"And we will. That's what our planning is for. I'll need you to work on your investigation of those two. Coordinate with Emma. Bill will need whatever you find. For now, I'm off to find him and then Nollan. I need to get information from both of them." Richard walked away at that point.

Nollan turned from his back door that afternoon. He had quit work early, too troubled to concentrate. He had been to the surgeon that morning. The good news that he desperately needed had come from that man. He could finally get rid of the sling and start physiotherapy. Nollan was happy to leave the sling behind. That freed him up to work better.

His thoughts turned to Naomi. He had plans for Friday night. He just prayed that they would be able to fulfill their plans for dinner and a walk. Nollan turned as he heard the doorbell, walking through. He stared at Richard who stood there.

"Richard? What are you doing here?" Nollan pointed towards the living room. "Can I get you anything?"

"No, I'm fine, Nollan. We need to talk."

"I gathered that or you would not be here. Just tell me. Naomi is okay?" Nollan held his breath until Richard nodded.

"She is. I'm sure that she's looking for you to come and find her. We need to talk, as I said. We've been working as a team to come up with plans to try and keep the two of you safe. I've spoken to two friends who have security teams. We work together as we need to."

Nollan nodded, having assumed that at some point, it would come to this.

"I thought something like this would come to pass. What can I do?" Nollan leaned back in his chair, his eyes not moving from Richard.

"What can you do? First, pray. That is the most important thing. And I understand that you have been. Second? Be aware of who is around you at all times. You won't pick up on everyone. It's not possible to do that without training. Even as well trained as we are, we can miss people. That's why we always work as a team. That one person could be the one that kills you.

"Third, work with us. Let us keep you safe. If that means I put one of my team with you during the day, I'll do that. It won't be Naomi. You are too close to her and she is too close to you. We can all see that you are starting to have feelings for her. I read her that she is having feelings for you."

Nollan hesitated for a moment, not saying a word. His feelings had to be discussed with that lady first. Richard nodded to himself. He would have felt the same way.

Chapter 20

Nollan reached for Naomi's hand on the Friday night as they walked towards the Italian restaurant near the water. It was a favourite of both of them. Naomi had a huge smile on her face. She was happy, despite the uncertainty in which she and Nollan found themselves.

Nollan had spent the last few days deep in an investigation that was puzzling him. There should be no good reason for it. He could find nothing wrong. If what he was being told was true, then there should be. He had reached out to Bill that day, giving him the name of the company and his lack of findings. Nollan looked down at Naomi, a grin on his own face. He too was happy, with the woman who he finally acknowledged that he loved.

Their meal completed, Nollan reached for Naomi's hand, leading her to the path by the river. This was also a favourite spot for both of them, now something else that they shared.

Naomi drew in a deep breath. She didn't want to ruin their night but she needed to talk with Nollan. Nollan was watching her and sighed as well.

"Naomi, set aside your worries for the night. We'll talk in the morning. For now, just relax and enjoy the evening." He reached to kiss her temple.

Naomi snuggled closer to him. Nollan made her feel cherished. However, she could still feel someone stalking them, watching their every move. That disturbed her a lot. She had spoken with the three of her team mates that had gone through this. And she had spoken to their spouses. Their responses, even though she had been expecting them, had not helped her feel any better.

Nollan waited until he heard Naomi lock her door before he headed back for his truck. He was deeply disturbed that night, fearing for her. He really didn't care about himself. He just prayed for protection for her, for healing for himself. Richard had sent him a text message which he finally read. He nodded. Nollan was aware that someone was around. He had caught glimpses of a form staking out his business and his home. Bill had been called, searched, and then just shrugged. There was no evidence to show who it was. And without that, they could not make any arrests.

The next morning, Benjamin watched as Nollan and Naomi mingled with her family. Michael had joined them at his request. He had felt that they needed to get to know Nollan's family. It would appear that Nollan would be in their family to stay. He turned as he felt Eve's hand tuck into his.

"She's happy, Benjamin." Eve was watching their daughter.

"She is. And he is too. God brought them together. I just wish that it had been under different circumstances. God knows best. We have to accept that."

"We do. We also need to make a trip to his aunt's tea room. We haven't been in a while. Now that it seems that he's going to be part of our family, we need to reach out to her."

"And we will. Has Naomi said anything about what she's going through?" Benjamin had not had a chance to speak with his daughter.

"No, she hasn't. I think that she is avoiding us right at the moment. We'll need to find time to talk with both of them before they leave. And somehow I think that will be difficult."

Benjamin began to laugh, the resigned look on his wife's face setting him off. They knew their youngest daughter only too well. If she didn't want to speak about something, then she wouldn't.

Naomi's head had raised as she heard her mother laughing, catching her eye. She nodded in agreement. She was happy, she knew, but also deeply worried about what they were facing. She had worked in security too long to be blindfolded to that.

Nollan turned from speaking with Nora, finding Nora's young son clutching at the leg of his jeans. He looked down at the toddler, finding the little one with his arms raised, not giving him a choice as to whether or not he would deny him that. Gathered into Nollan's arms, the little fellow simply hugged him and then gave him a sloppy kiss. Nollan was surprised at that and looked at him with a grin. Naomi moved closer to him, a grin on her face as well.

"He does that, Nollan." Naomi's hand was out to touch her little nephew. "I didn't think to warn you."

"It's okay." Nollan looked around at the group that had gathered. He found Michael talking with Naomi's brothers-in-law. "You have a great family."

"I do. I'm not comfortable being around them right now, but I have to. I'm not sure if that makes any sense."

"It does. We still have to have that talk, you know." Nollan studied her, seeing the fear that she was trying hard to hide.

"I know. And Mom and Dad want that talk as well. You're troubled." Naomi was beginning to read him.

"You're right. I am. I worry about you when I'm not with you." Nollan was putting his heart out there, he knew, not sure if he should at this point. He didn't remove his eyes from her, finding her staring at him.

"I think we need more than one talk, then, Nollan." Naomi walked away at a call from Nora, leaving him staring after her.

Benjamin moved to stand beside the younger man, finding his grandson reaching for him. Taking him, he spoke quietly to him before he set him down on the floor, watching as he headed for his cousin.

"Nollan? How are you really doing? You've healed?"

"I am healing, Benjamin. I'm starting physiotherapy next week which will help. But that is not what you're asking."

"No, it's not. We need to talk, Nollan. I need to know as much of what is going on that you can give us." Benjamin would not pry but he knew that the younger man would share what he could. "Come with me then. Eve will come and find us. It's almost lunchtime. I know that you want to be back on the road while you still have daylight to get home."

Nollan found Naomi beside him as he stared at her father. Reaching for her hand, he followed Benjamin to his study, seating Naomi and then sitting beside her. He kept his eyes on Benjamin, bowing his head as the older man began to pray.

They talked for a while, the younger couple not able to share a lot. Benjamin nodded. He was aware that they had given what they could.

Chapter 21

Nollan watched carefully around his truck as he drove home in the late afternoon. Naomi was quiet but still watching as well. She felt uncomfortable, just as she always did when danger was unknown but close to her. She hated that the feeling was coming at the end of a wonderful day spent with her family.

"Nollan? You were okay with Dad speaking as he did?" She turned her head to watch him.

"I am, love. I am. I would have done the same had I been in your father's place. You're his daughter. He will look out for you no matter how old you are."

"I know. I just wish that he would not this time. It's too dangerous for him and Mom." Naomi was frustrated that her father was not backing down from her this time.

"He won't. He is well aware that you are an adult and very capable of taking care of yourself." Nollan slowed to turn into a coffee shop. "How be we grab a coffee for me and a tea for you?"

Naomi nodded, watching the traffic around her. One truck followed them. She pulled out her phone and took a photo of it. It had been following them, hanging back just far enough that she could not see the occupants.

Nollan walked back towards the truck, carrying their drinks. His eyes narrowed as he saw the truck that had pulled in after him. It had been following him, he knew. He was concerned but shrugged it off for the moment.

Handing Naomi her tea, Nollan didn't immediately start up his truck. He sat, his thoughts muddled for a moment. He reached for her hand, bowing his head to pray for them both. Naomi followed with her own prayer. He didn't release her hand. Instead, his hand tightened on hers.

"Naomi, we have not known each other all that long. We have been thrown into something that we don't understand at the moment. God is with us. He is protecting us in ways that we don't see. What I want to say? You are a beautiful, compassionate, giving lady. I am honoured to call you my friend. Now, I have a question for you. Are you willing to go out with me? Consider yourself my lady?" He didn't look at her. He didn't want to see rejection on her face.

Naomi had not taken her eyes from him as he spoke. She was relieved, she decided, knowing where he stood. She felt the same way. She tugged at his hand, bringing his eyes to her.

"I will, Nollan. I will consider myself your lady." She gave a gentle smile. "God has brought us together. He will guide us as we move forward." She sipped at her tea before she spoke again. "And we know that it will get more and more dangerous."

Nollan agreed with her statement. It would just get worse and worse. That he knew only too well from his conversations with her team and with Bill.

———

"God is good, my love. He'll be there with us every step of the way." Nollan reached to start the truck, driving off.

The truck that had been following him pulled out as well. Neither Nollan nor Naomi say it. They were deep in conversation. Laughter filled the truck cab. They didn't realize that it would get worse for them in the following days.

Naomi walked through her home that evening, a dreamy look on her face. Nollan had dropped her off and then headed for his own home. She was still uneasy, though. Something bad was about to happen. She knew better than to ignore it, no matter what she was feeling.

Richard reached for his phone. He had tried to reach out to Naomi that afternoon but had not heard back from her. He needed to talk with her, preferably as soon as possible. That was not happening, he decided, sending her off a text instead. He would catch up with her if not on the morrow, then on Monday. All he could do was pray for her. Richard heard the chime for a text message and pulled it up. Naomi had responded, simply stating that she had been out of town. Did he want her to call him now? His response was no, that they would talk on Monday.

Nollan stared at his computer screen late that night. He was not prepared for what he had just found. An investigation that he had been running was completed. He shoved back his chair and paced, his eyes returning again and again to his computer screen. This was not what he had expected to find. This meant that the work the company was doing was dangerous to the workers. He couldn't leave it. On the other hand, he could not go to the company when he was not sure who all was involved. He finally just walked away. This was something that he needed to pray over. He would also need to speak with the authorities. That would not happen that night.

Bill walked slowly through the department building that night. He was on call and always dreaded weekends. This weekend had been no different. He had been called in to a murder scene. Handed the wallet of the deceased man, he opened it, pausing as he read the name. This was not who he had expected. He would need to speak with Naomi and her family. The man who had murdered her grandfather was now a murder victim himself. He dropped into his desk chair, knowing that he needed to work through this that night but exhausted. Reaching for a calendar, Bill studied it. He was due for a vacation in the next two weeks, once he made it through that weekend. He was looking forward to getting away with Cora and their young son, Michael. That meant that he would need to speak with Andrew tomorrow and also Naomi.

The man watching Naomi's home shook his head. He had been there all day, not finding her outside like she normally was. There had been no sign of any activity at all. That was until now when low lights shone behind the closed drapes. He was angry. His instructions had been to find her that day and bring her to his employer. He had a good idea why, having overheard conversation that he should not have heard. It troubled him to some extent but crime had hardened him to the point that he no longer cared about people. They were just commodities to him.

———

The man walked away at last, knowing that he would not be able to break into her home. She had it too well secured. He would be back on the morrow. And he was determined to succeed. He didn't see the neighbour who stood in the dark, watching the watcher. That man had watched the car that had not moved all day and that didn't belong to anyone in the neighbour. He had taken careful note of the license plate. The neighbour fingered the paper, knowing that he needed to call it in. He walked back into his house, picked up his phone, and called the non-emergency line for the police department. Explaining who his neighbour was and what he had observed, he was taken seriously. The dispatcher promised that they would take care of it for him. Patrol vehicles were dispatched to search for the car, not finding it.

Chapter 22

Bill tracked down Naomi on the Sunday afternoon. She took one look at him and walked back through her house. She didn't like the look on his face. Bill carefully shut the door and followed her.

"Naomi? We need to talk."

"I get that. We need to. But do we want to?" Naomi turned to face him her arms wrapping around her abdomen.

"The man who murdered your grandfather? I was called to a murder scene last night. It was him." Bill watched as her eyes slid closed before they popped open.

"He was? That ends that, doesn't it? But it doesn't end this. You now need to find out who that was and why. I'm not safe yet. We don't know who is after us. I spoke with my neighbour this morning. He was waiting for me. He reported a vehicle that had been parked on our street all day. It was not one that belonged here."

Bill stared at her before he nodded. He had received that report that morning and had spoken with the neighbour.

"I see. Your neighbours are taking care of you, aren't they?" He paced her kitchen, trying to come up with a way to protect her and not finding that. "How do we proceed then in keeping you safe?"

"It's not just me, Bill. It's Nollan as well. How do we keep him safe? Have you spoken with him today? He was looking for you. He has something that he needs to give you. That's why he's not here right now. He dropped me off at home and then headed downtown. Nollan was then heading for the department to try and find you or Lily."

Bill stopped his pacing, his eyes on Naomi. Something had changed between Naomi and Nollan, he sensed. Just what that was, he wasn't sure.

"I see. I'll track him down. You need to be very careful, Naomi."

"I know that, Bill, as you are well aware. Now, head off and find Nollan." Naomi locked the door behind him, walking back through to the kitchen, and then out of the back door to her favourite seat on her porch. Her head bowed as she prayed and wept. Her emotions were in a turmoil from so many causes. This was not Naomi to give in. She had reached her breaking point and could only reach for the hem of the garment for healing.

Nollan turned from the front desk in the police department. He was frustrated. He had been told that Bill was not in the office at the moment but was expected back shortly. Nollan just wanted to speak with him. Only he was not around.

Walking down the steps to the sidewalk, Nollan hesitated before he just sat. Bill walked out of the door a few moments later, staring at him before he walked down the steps to sit beside him.

———

"Waiting for something, Nollan?" Bill's voice was quiet. He stared ahead, not sure why Nollan was there. He knew that the other man had been looking for him, and he himself had gone on a search for him.

"I am, Bill. I need to talk with you about a company that I took an assignment for. I should not have found anything but I did. That's concerning enough that I have not back to the company. I am stalling them for now." He handed over a flash drive. "This is what I've found. If this company continues with its work, it will cause harm or injury to its workers. If this gets out into the community, the repercussions could be grave." Nollan was on his feet as he finished, walking way from Bill.

Bill stood, his eyes on Nollan as he drove away before he looked down at the piece of plastic that he held. He didn't need this, not the day before his vacation. But dedicated to his work, he found his office and looked at the material that Nollan had provided. He copied it to his computer and then was on his feet, hunting for the one detective who had experience in that line of investigation. He handed over the flash drive with a quiet word. The woman nodded and took it, knowing that it would add to her work.

Nollan simply wrapped his sweetheart into his arms. She was upset, he could tell. Traces of tears still showed on her face. He prayed for her before he asked what had happened.

Naomi hugged him harder, hearing his prayer for her. She was beginning to know the man who was holding her.

———

"Nollan, did you find Bill?" She leaned back to look up at him.

"I did. He took it. I have no idea what he will do with it. He assured me that he would look into it. I just wish that there was more that I could do. That company is putting people at risk." Nollan stared down at her as she shoved at him.

"There is something that we can do." Naomi grabbed his hand and pulled him with her. She shoved him down into her desk chair. "We can email Emma and see what she can find. And Silver's husband, Sorley, does financial investigations. I also know others who can help. One of my friends' father-in-law is a private investigator and he also does financial investigations. Another friend can do a family tree on whoever it is that is discovered. We are not alone in this investigation, Nollan."

Nollan stared at her, not sure what to think. He didn't realize that she had the resources that she did. He shook his head, knowing that he should have.

"Okay, Naomi. I just need to email them, correct?" Nollan looked up as she laughed. "Is that funny?" His eyes narrowed as he saw the laughter on her face and then realized what he had said. "I didn't phrase that very well, did I?"

"Not really. Pull up what you need to. I can give you their emails. Sunday or not, Emma will start her search. She has been in touch already about that man." Naomi's voice stilled. "That man? Nollan, you know that man that murdered my grandfather?"

Nollan looked up at the tone of her voice. It was not one that he had heard before. He really couldn't describe it other than it held fear.

"Why about him?" Nollan waited patiently for her to speak. "Naomi? What about that man?"

"Bill was around here early this morning. That man was murdered. And they have no information on who or why. And then a neighbour approached me this morning before you came. He reported a strange vehicle parked on my street."

"He did? Your neighbours are taking care of you." Nollan reached to hug her.

"They are, Nollan. They are. I pray that your neighbours will as well. My block is well known to each other. We gather every couple of months for a potluck. That's coming up soon before the kids get back to school."

"I'm coming with you." Nollan's attention went back to the emails that he was composing, missing the look on Naomi's face.

Naomi realized that Nollan had just put himself more directly into her life. She glowed for a moment before she turned and walked away, to turn and stare at him.

Chapter 23

Richard was on the hunt for Naomi. She was not in the office building. He headed for the training building, thinking that would be where he found her. Her car was still there. Richard searched the building for her.

Stephen stood for a moment, watching Richard before he approached him.

"Richard? You're looking for one of us?"

"I am." Richard walked towards him. "Have you seen her?"

"I did. She and Silver went on a food run. They should be back shortly." Stephen pointed at his watch. "It is almost lunchtime."

"It is. I hadn't realized that it had gotten so late. Stephen, what is your reading on Naomi right now?"

Stephen had been expecting that question. Richard would check in on each one of them every week. It had happened more so with what they had gone through. Richard wasn't just their employer. He was a friend and brother in Christ to each one of them.

"Naomi? She's hurting, Richard. And she's not sharing. I wish that she would. It's hard to know how to help her."

Richard pointed towards his house. "We'll eat on the back porch today I think." He waved at Timothy who was in the process of locking the office building doors. The team that they were training had been in and gone for the day, due back in on the next day.

Richard assessed each one of his team. He was constantly doing that, knowing that their health was something that he needed to be on top of. Each one affected the other. He nodded as he did that. They were doing well, but he frowned as he studied Naomi. She was somewhat withdrawn that day. He would find out why, if she would just stay in one spot for him to do so.

"Naomi?" Richard's voice stopped her as she moved away. "Can we talk?"

Naomi sighed. She had tried to avoid him but knew that she would be unable to. It had been unfair of her to even attempt it.

"You want to talk." Naomi returned to sit at the outside table, her eyes on him. "I'm okay, Richard. Well, as okay as I can be in these situations." She grinned briefly as he laughed. "But there have been some changes."

Richard reached for the pad of paper and pen that he had handy. He would make notes and then decide from there how to proceed.

"Go ahead, Naomi. What do you have to tell me?"

"First, the man who murdered my grandfather has been murdered. Bill does not have a lot of information on that. Also, Nollan has found something disturbing in one of his investigations. He has reached out to others to help. Bill has also been advised. But with Bill away on holidays, we're not sure where that stands."

Richard nodded. He had been aware that Bill was away on vacation for the next two weeks. He had prayed that whatever it was that Naomi was facing would be over. Only, it wasn't. That disturbed him.

"Tell him to call me and let me know what we can do for him. I am assuming that Emma would be one of the people that you referred him to." Richard smiled at her nod. "Now, Naomi, let me pray for you. We need to do that."

"I know, Richard. I have been doing that but sometimes it's hard to trust. When someone is after you and you don't know who, it makes you distrust everyone."

"It does, Naomi. That's where our faith comes in. We've had this discussion many times."

'We have Richard. I just wish that I could do more." Naomi rose, walked away, and climbed into her car. She drove away, Richard standing on his porch and watching her.

Lord, be with my friend. Protect her. Help us to solve this. Give us the wisdom that we need. Thank you, Lord. Love You.

Nollan stood on his front yard that afternoon, watching as police officers moved around his home and then in and out of it. He had arrived home to find his front door shattered to pieces, his security system in shambles, and his house ransacked. His computer had been thrown on the floor, breaking it. He was thankful that he always backed his work up and locked that backup away when he was out of the house.

Lily beckoned to him, causing him to finally move. He had felt that he was frozen in place. He didn't realize that Naomi had appeared, called there by Lily, her hand reaching for his. He only knew that he was not alone.

"Nollan? Your place is a mess, to put it lightly. Can you tell me if you notice any missing at the moment?" Lily walked through it with him.

Nollan stood in his office, staring at his computer. He sighed to himself. This what not what he needed, not at all.

"Not right away, Lily. I'll need to go over everything and see if there is anything gone." He felt a tug at his hand, surprised to find Naomi there and then grateful that she was.

"We'll work on cleaning it up. I've called in reinforcements, Lily. You're on duty, correct?"

Lily glanced at her watch.

"I am and I need to get on the move. Call me, Nollan, with what is missing." She walked away, leaving Nollan staring at the mess and Naomi staring at him.

Naomi walked away from him, somewhat reluctantly, as she heard Richard. Richard stared at the mess.

"What happened, Naomi?"

"I don't know. Lily called me to come. This is what I found. Nollan is in shock, to put it mildly. I'm staying to help him clean up. But it's going to take a while."

Richard nodded before his phone was out. A group text reached out to a number of their friends, who all pledged to come and help them.

"I've called in some of our friends. We'll have it tidy in no time. But Nollan will need to be aware that he needs to tell us what is missing."

Nollan had approached, hearing Richard's voice.

"I can do that, Richard. This is not what I wanted to come home to. And the security system is a mess."

"My guys will look after that. Stephen asked about that. He'll grab what he needs and repair it. Now, where do we start?"

Nollan shrugged, not sure. Naomi walked away, heading for his kitchen. Her steps stopped before she headed for the fridge. It seemed okay, she decided, not tampered with. It seems that whoever it was had been looking for something that they could not find.

Chapter 24

Looking around his house late that night, Nollan was grateful for Richard calling in his friends, all of whom now claimed him as theirs. Adam, a contractor, had found a door to replace the one that had been shattered. He had waved away Nollan's offer to pay, simply stating that's what they did for friends. And they were friends, were they not?

Naomi had just left, the last one to go. He had hugged her, hanging on tightly, not wanting to let her walk away. He was deeply afraid for her, afraid that something would happen to her. He was learning to let God have his worries. That had been a lifelong problem for him. He wanted to hold them and not let them go. His aunt and cousin had tried to convince him of that but he had just shaken his head and walked away from them.

He walked through his house, seeing that the debris had disappeared. Pictures had been taken for his insurance company. The agent had shown up at one point, talking with him, taking his own photos, and then disappearing. Nollan had no idea that there would be so many people in and out of his house. He was grateful for their help. Nollan was more grateful for the way that they had taken time, each one of them, man or lady, to stop and pray with him. That would help get him through what he needed to.

His steps took him to his office where he stood, staring at the spot that should house his computer. He frowned. A new computer and monitor stood there. He reached for the sticky note.

Richard had taken Silver with him, heading for a friend's store. He had put in his request and the friend had nodded. He had just that computer in stock and would willingly let Nollan have it for what it cost him.

Nollan blinked rapidly, tears clouding his sight for a moment. He had not expected Richard to do that, but then again, that was Richard. Richard took care of his friends, stepping in as he needed to and stepping back when he had to. This was one time he had felt God's nudge to step in.

Reaching for his phone, Nollan sent off a quick thank you text to Richard. He smiled at Richard's return text of simply a welcome. He had made more friends in the last weeks in this town than he had in all the years that he had lived here. He knew that it was Naomi. Naomi was drawing him into her group of friends, friends that he knew cared about one another.

Walking back through his house, Nollan rubbed at his arm and the collarbone. Both were aching tonight. He had not been allowed to do any lifting or minimal lifting if that. He was grateful for that. He was aware that he would not have been able to clean the house up that quickly if it had been on his own.

He frowned as he heard a tap at the door and walked that way, peeking out before he opened the door.

"Michael? What are you doing here? It's late." Nollan closed and locked the door. As he did so, he saw the duffle bag in his cousin's hand. "What's this?"

———

128

"I'm staying with you for now. Mom had a bad feeling tonight that you were in trouble. She wasn't able to get through to you."

"I know. I sent her a text message just a bit ago. Thanks, cuz. I can use the company."

"What happened, Nollan? I know that something did." Michael walked through Nollan's home, seeing items missing. "You're missing things."

"I know I am. I had a break-in at some point this afternoon. Naomi and her friends appeared and helped clean up." Nollan yawned, suddenly exhausted. "That still doesn't explain you."

"I told you. Mom had that feeling. You know? That one where she's convinced something is going to happen to one of us?"

"Yeah, I know that feeling. I wish that she had been wrong." Nollan yawned before he headed for the kitchen. "I have coffee on the go. I won't be sleeping yet."

"No, I don't expect that you will. Nollan? Naomi? Is she the one?" Michael hesitated to intrude into his cousin's life. Nollan and he were close enough to be brothers so he felt he had no choice but to ask.

"The one? The one that we want in our lives? The love of our lives that we're waiting for? The lady who God planned for us?" Nollan turned to face his cousin. At his nod, Nollan rubbed at his face. He wasn't quite sure how to answer. "She may be, Michael. We're dating. And you know that I don't date."

"Neither of us do. We were waiting for the one. I watched you two the other day. You're two parts of a whole." Michael swiped his cousin's mug. "But that's not all."

"No, it's not. I found some information on a company that friends are looking into for me. I have also gone to Bill about it. It's very disturbing, Michel. Very disturbing."

"And is that why your house was tossed like this?" Michael looked around the kitchen before heading for the mudroom and then back. "They've damaged some things."

"They have. A friend is coming through tomorrow to assess what we need to do. He's a contractor."

"Must be a new friend."

"He is. Adam is a friend of Naomi's. Richard called in their friend group and all of them showed up. I think at one point I had about two dozen people in my house. It's no wonder that we were able to clean it up and set it back to rights." Nollan studied his mug. He had never had that large of a group of friends. He was still shaken by the invasion. Having had each one pray for him had helped to some extent. He knew that it would take time to get over it

"You'll get there, cuz. Now, what can I do for you?" Michael snuck a glance at the clock. It wasn't midnight yet.

"I really don't know. To tell the truth, Michael, I feel threatened and stalked and at a loss. I want to protect Naomi. Only thing? She's much better at protecting me than the other way around."

"Yeah, given her work, she would be. Has she said anything about you having to go into hiding?"

"Richard briefly mentioned it. He's working through some plans, he tells me, that he hopes never to have to use. He also has two friends with security teams that he'll pull in, he said, if he needs to. Naomi sources out safe houses for them. She is apparently working on that."

"It sounds as if he is thinking ahead." Michael opened the fridge door and then closed it. He knew that if he was hungry, he could help himself to the food. He just wasn't hungry. He was worried about his cousin.

"Michael? Say what you are thinking." Nollan stood with a half grin on his face, facing his cousin. A hand came out to hold the fridge door closed.

Michael began to laugh, Nollan's wording common phrases for the both of them.

"Say what I think? You really want to know?" At Nollan's nod, Michael smirked. "I think that you should just marry Naomi. You're in love with her. That would make it much easier to keep the two of you safe." Michael walked away, the smirk still on his face.

Nollan stared after him, the look on his face saying that Michael was right. That was exactly what he wanted to do. Only he couldn't. Not yet at any rate.

Chapter 25

Nollan hesitated the next morning, finding Lily waiting at his office building. He had not expected to see her again that quickly.

"Lily? Do you need to see me?" Nollan unlocked the door and switched off the security system. He looked around quickly. Nothing seemed to be out of order here.

"I do. I have some questions about the break-in at your home. Do you have time to speak with me now?" Lily followed him in, doing her own assessment of the office.

"I do. My secretary's off today, so my time is limited. What do you need to know?" Nollan dropped his briefcase on his desk and walked back towards Lily.

"First, did you find anything missing?"

"Missing? Not a thing. Did I find things destroyed? A lot of things. Nothing that I really cared about personally. The major thing destroyed was my computer."

"And that makes it difficult for you if you want to work from home? Do you work from home a lot?" Lily watched Nollan closely, alert for any clue that would tell her that he was lying or hiding something.

"I sometimes do. But my work is always backed up. I lock the backup away. I don't just leave it on my computer. My computer is encrypted and the passwords are as strong as I can make them.”

“Okay, so they can’t stop you from that. They did destroy your computer.” She stared at him as he grinned.

“That one. Richard reached out to a friend and I have one that’s even better than the one that was destroyed. It was brought in last night.”

Lily nodded, knowing Richard had a huge circle of friends, some closer than others.

“You were surprised. It’s what Richard does. He takes care of us all.”

“He does. He needs a lady in his life.” Nollan grinned as Lily began to laugh.

“He does. We tell him that all the time. His response is that he’s waiting on God’s timing and the lady who God has planned for him.”

“That’s the way to look at it.” Nollan perched himself on the corner of the desk in the office area. “Lily? Can I ask you something?”

“Sure. I may or may not be able to answer your question.”

“That’s fair. I am at a loss to know who would be after me. I mean, I do research and investigations. Those findings go back to the company that hired me. I don’t go any further with what I find. Except for that one that I passed on to Bill.”

"He mentioned it in passing. Andrea is working on it. What's your question?" Lily dropped into one of the upholstered chairs.

Nollan wasn't quite sure how to frame his question. He didn't know Lily all that well.

"Bear with me. I'm thinking aloud. I talk to myself a lot." He grinned as she laughed at him. "Okay. So I was with Naomi when her car exploded. We had never met before then. I stepped in as a friend that day. You know what all has happened. I don't know if I have any enemies. I may do related to my work. I am an orphan, as you know. I think you've picked my brain about my life.

"I have no answers as to who this may be that is after me. Naomi and I have gone over as much as we can of everything that I can think of. Between Naomi and her friends, I think they know every thought or idea that I have ever had. How do I do this? How do I find out who is it?"

"That's a good question, Nollan. I'm not sure that we can give you an answer for that. Whoever it is that is after you and apparently after Naomi at the same time is hiding. They are not sending either one of you the letters or the packages that we would normally be seeing. Your home was destroyed. We don't know if it was them or someone random." Lily held up her hand as Nollan opened his mouth to speak. "We don't, Nollan. We found very little evidence last night when the team went through. Given that your computer was destroyed, that shows anger to some extent as does other items being destroyed."

"I get that, Lily. I really do. I'm just afraid that I will bring danger to someone I love or one of my friends. And that I want to avoid." He paused, rubbing at his cheek for a moment before he crossed his arms again across his chest.

"We understand that, Nollan. We truly do. We've seen this with too many of our friends. I can guarantee you that the group that was pulled in was a group of eight couples." At his nod, she smiled. "They all faced things, danger, abductions, what have you. They survived and became closer as a couple. Their faith also increased.

"Now, as to how to keep you safe? That's a good question. For starters, vary the times that you leave for work and return to work. Don't stay shut up in here all day. Leave. Come back. Go home. Go visit someone. Go out for a meal. Spend time with your friends. They will welcome you without worrying about any danger that you think you may bring to them.

"Be as vigilant as you can when you are out. I know that's tough. You'll tell me that you don't know who to look for. No, you won't. Just be aware of who is around you at all times. If you feel something off, find somewhere safe to wait until an officer can reach you.

"This is, I know, hard to do. It is with everyone that faces this. I would suggest that you spend time with Naomi. She can teach you how to be vigilant and what to watch for in a general manner. Richard's team is one of the best that I know. He has two friends that are just as good. If he feels it becomes necessary, then he will stick you away somewhere, either with his team or one of the others. Does this help?"

"It does, Lily. I know that we can't totally avoid everything. I would like to do that as much as I can. Is there anything else that you need to ask me?"

"Not really. I just wanted to touch base with you and see how you were doing. It is a shock what you faced last night. It is not the way that you want to find your home. Timothy and Stephen were able to reinstall your security system?"

"They were." Nollan was on his feet, walking out with Lily. "Stay safe, Lily. You have a dangerous occupation. You are a good friend to Naomi. I could use you as a friend as well. I don't want to see any harm come to you."

Nollan watched as she drove away, his head tilting up as he felt the sun on his face. It felt good. It felt, he decided, as if he had been inside a deep long dark tunnel or in the midst of a storm and was finally reaching the end of the journey. He just didn't know how the journey would end.

Chapter 26

Lily tracked down Naomi that afternoon. She had gone off duty and just wanted to spend some time with her friend. Naomi opened the door, beckoned her in, and pointed to the kitchen. Her phone was tucked between her ear and her shoulder as she made notes. Lily dropped the bag of food on the table and reached for the kettle. She needed a cup of tea, and she knew that Naomi would want one as well.

Naomi set her phone done, disturbed by Emma's call. She had information that she needed to think about and then absorb. She would also need to speak with Nollan. Emma had indicated that she would be sending the same information on to Nollan. Would she be speaking with him, Emma had inquired, a laugh in her voice. Naomi had made a comment that she would be, at some point.

Turning as she heard Naomi, Lily reached to hug her friend before she pointed at their food.

"I wanted some junk food tonight. I'm hoping that you do as well."

"I do. Thank you, Lily. It's my turn next time."

"Sure." Lilly watched her friend closely. Something was going on with her, she decided, but she didn't know how to ask her.

"Lily? Where does the investigation stand? Are you close to finding the culprits?" Naomi was hopeful that they were.

"No, I'm sorry, Naomi. We're not. We just don't have enough information. We're working on it but for now, without that piece of information that we need, we can't move forward very quickly."

"I know. I was hoping that you had." Naomi dropped her burger back on the wrapper. "I'm just tired of this."

"I understand. All our victims feel the same." Lily observed the jump that Naomi gave. "You are a victim, Naomi. Just like the ones who you used to guard. Just like your friends. Just like your team mates. Have you talked to anyone yet?"

Naomi nodded, not saying who she was counselling with.

"I am. I am. I wish that I didn't have to."

"But you need to. It will help get you through this."

Lily rose at last, heading for home. It had been a long day, and tomorrow promised to be that much longer. She hesitated as she walked to her front door. She reached for the letter, finding a note from Old George. Lily nodded. She would track him down on the next day.

Nollan turned his face up to the night sky. His eyes closed as he felt the soft breeze crossing his face. He heard the night sounds and found himself relaxing. It had been a stressful day for him. The company CEO had called him, asking for a report. He had put him off, not sure how to respond.

———

His phone vibrated but he ignored it. There were times that he had to go no contact with everyone and set any electronics to one side. Tonight was one of those nights. He knew that his family and friends would just leave or text a message to him.

He rose at last to head inside. He didn't hear the soft footsteps behind him as he closed and locked the door, turning off lights as he headed for his rest.

The man who had been watching him reached for him, his hands missing him as the door closed. His hands clenched as he cursed under his breath. He needed to bring Nollan to a certain address. That was to have been that night. It had taken him time to track Nollan down and then to work carefully around to the back of the house, hoping to find an unlocked door. He had been taken aback to see Nollan sitting there. He had been careful to approach, working his way slowly towards him.

Pulling out his phone, Nollan scrolled through his messages and responded to those that he needed to. He stopped on the message from Naomi. It was just a good night text, stating that she was praying for him. His face softened as he responded. He was in love with this lady.

Naomi set her phone on her night stand and pulled the covers up to her ears. She was asleep before she ever realized it, waking in the morning refreshed. She reached for her phone, a smile on her face. Nollan had sent a good morning text. The hearts attached to it caught her attention. Did he really mean that?

On her feet, she headed for the front door, stopping suddenly. Something was off there, she felt, and headed for the back door. She slid to a stop there as well. She couldn't go out of that door. Reaching for her phone, Naomi called Lily.

"Lily? Where are you?"

"Just heading out of my door. Why?"

"There's something wrong outside of my house. Something about both doors. I don't feel that I can go out of them." Naomi ran for her office, knowing that the window there was somewhat hidden and she would be able to drop down behind bushes.

"Naomi? Get out of your house! Now!" Lily's call to their dispatch sent patrol officers heading Naomi's way just as Lily was. Lily slammed her car door, running around the house, looking for her friend.

Naomi was on her feet as she saw Lily, running towards her. Lily grabbed at her arm, pulling her towards her vehicle and shoving her inside. She pointed at the house as officers poured out of their vehicles.

The officers searched the property, hesitating as they approached both the front door and the back door. One motioned for Lily, who moved rapidly towards him.

"Lily? That's a bomb. And it's attached to the door knob. And Joe says it's the same as the back door. How did she not open the door"

"Her training and instincts. She can read situations and react. This was no different. Richard's team is good at this. This training and awareness of their surroundings have saved them on multiple occasions." Lily turned to find Naomi watching her from the car. "I'll need to talk with her. You've called in the bomb squad?"

"I have, Lily. Some of us will be here for a while. Head off with Naomi." He walked away, heading back for the front porch, to stand facing the street, eyes watching for anyone who didn't belong.

"Lily? What was there?" Naomi's eyes shifted between Lily and her home.

"Bombs, Naomi. Bombs at both doors. If you had moved the door knob, you would be dead." Lily didn't pull her punches with Naomi. She knew better than to do that.

Naomi looked at her and then at her home. Her eyes closed. Her home was not safe.

"Can you take me to work? I'm needed there today."

Lily nodded, knowing that was what Naomi would want.

Richard paused as he walked towards the office building. He was not expecting to see Lily out there but she was. She was, in fact, waiting for him to approach.

"Lily? Is there a reason that you're out here?" Richard stopped beside her, searching her face, seeing the anger in her. "Which one?"

"Naomi." Lily knew exactly what Richard was asking. "Talk to her. She's shaken worse than I have ever been her."

"Talk to me. Tell me what happened."

"She tried to leave her home this morning and had a strong feeling that she could not open either the front door or the back door. She called me and then jumped out of a window and hid until I go there. There was a bomb at her front door and one at her back door. I talked to the bomb squad just to confirm what the patrol officer stated. If she had just turned the door knob a bit, the bomb would have exploded. She would not have survived."

Richard paled, not sure that he was hearing Lily correctly. He stared at her and then at the office building.

"You brought her out here." That was a statement and not a question.

"I did. She needed to be here. You'll keep her safe over the day. We'll need to figure out something for tonight. She can't go back to her home. But I know that she will want that. I'll head back that way. She's given me her spare key."

"Thank you, Lily. Keep us updated on what you find."

"I will do that, Richard. Now, go find her. And she needs to talk to Nollan. He needs to watch out for bombs as well." Lily disappeared, leaving Richard studying the gravel on the driveway before he headed for the office.

Richard walked through the building slowly, processing what Lily had told him. He sat at his desk, working through what he needed to. Timothy and Silver were training today. Stephen had needed the day off for personal reasons. That left only Naomi and himself in the office.

He rose at last, heading for Naomi. He waited in the hallway until she had finished the phone call that she was on before he entered her office and sat. He just sat silent, knowing that Naomi would speak when she was ready to.

"Richard? Lily found you." Naomi blew out a breath, frustration evident. There was also fear underlying it as well.

"She stopped me on the way in. Naomi, what are we to do with you?" Richard asked that half in jest but mostly seriously.

"I have no idea, Richard. I really don't. I didn't expect to have those bombs set. And before you ask, I didn't hear anyone at all. I slept very soundly last night. Everything had caught up to me."

"It does that, Naomi. We've seen it many times over the years. You know that Lily is recommending that you not go home tonight."

Naomi nodded, already having had that conversation with Lily.

"That's her recommendation. I'm not being chased from my home, Richard. I won't let whoever it is have that much control over me. I can't." Naomi was almost in tears, something that Richard had rarely seen.

"That's about what I thought that you would say. How do we keep you safe? This was meant to kill you today, Naomi." Richard frowned as she stared at him.

"It was overkill, Richard. Why set two bombs? One would have been sufficient. Who is trying to threaten and kill me with bombs?"

"We don't know that, Naomi. You have as much information or more than we do. We'll need to meet again as a team and try and work it through."

"We will. This is so hard, you know. I don't like being the victim." She glared at Richard as he laughed.

"No one does, Naomi. No one person gets up in the morning and decides that is the day that they want to play victim." He rubbed at his neck. "We can meet late this afternoon. Stephen won't be there. He and Shanli are out of town until late. Timothy and Tate and Silver and Sorley will be there. Your place, I take it?"

"Absolutely. And I will ask Nollan if he wants to be there. This seems to be affecting him as well."

"It is. It is difficult to decide which one of you is the actual target."

"I know. It is tough to determine that. Let me have what you can today before you leave." He paused, eying her. "You don't have a vehicle."

"No, I don't." Naomi sounded disgruntled. "Lily didn't give me a choice this morning. She just drove off"

"Because she couldn't let you near your car. It may have had a bomb on it as well." Richard's hand was up to stop her words. "Just because it happened once doesn't mean that it can't happen again. Did you park in the garage last night?"

She looked grumpy at his question.

"No, I parked in the driveway. I didn't see the need to do that." She sighed, knowing what his next piece of advice would be. "And I need to do that, don't I ?"

"I would suggest that you do. It may mean the difference between staying alive and dying." Richard was blunt with her, but he knew Naomi well enough to know that he had to be.

"I know, Richard. I usually do. It's just that I was so tired last night. Lily brought a meal for us. I had intended to go out and move it and just forgot." Her head went down on her hands. "And that could have ended badly."

Richard didn't respond, just rose and walked away. Naomi heard his footsteps stop in his office before she looked up. Her chin rested on her hands as she thought about what had happened that day.

You were there, God. You stopped me from touching either door. You were there. You protected me in a way that I had not asked or ever expected to have that happen. Thank you, dear Father. Lead us in finding out who this is. We are at a dead end that seems to have no way to turn. You are in control, Lord. You know the path that I am walking and that Nollan is walking. You have brought us together. Hide us in the hollow. Cover us with Your hand. Protect our friends and families.

Chapter 28

Naomi looked around at her team mates who had gathered in her home that night. Nollan stood beside her, his arm around her shoulders. He didn't realize that he was claiming her as his own. The others understood what he wasn't saying in words.

"Richard? Where do we go now?" Timothy had his pen in his hand. "We need to figure this out."

"We do. We will. Naomi, has Lily said anything else to you?"

"About today? Not really. She left a voice mail asking me to be very careful. These bombs were really sophisticated from what she was told. I don't understand it at all, Richard. Who is doing this?" Naomi was puzzled and stressed. She felt Nollan's arm tighten around her as he sought to bring comfort to her.

"I don't know, Naomi. We've gone back over all of our cases. We've looked at your schooling and your family. We've gone back as far as we can. Emma has researched you until she says she can't research anything more. The same for Nollan."

"That's what she said. How do we do find out who it is?"

"That's the problem, isn't it, Richard?" Nollan moved away, returning with a folder that he had dropped onto the entry table. "Take a look at this. It may help. I have a company that I have found some information that is troubling. I have spoken with my lawyer. He says that there is not a problem for you to look into it." He handed the folder to Richard.

Richard took it, eying Nollan before he opened it. His hand froze as he did so. He knew the company. He had heard rumours about it for years. There had just not been any proof.

"I know this company, Nollan. There have been rumours for years about it. There has just never been any proof. You have it?"

Nollan hesitated for a moment before he nodded.

"I believe that I do. Some of it is there. I had found it and turned it over to Bill. Lily assures me that someone is investigating it. These investigations take time, unfortunately. That doesn't help us if they're the ones responsible for this."

"No, it doesn't. You have a lot of information here."

"I do. It's what I always do. That much research and investigation go into anything I do. I just don't look into the companies. I research their products. This is what I think triggered this for me. I hadn't planned on this much information being found. I don't like what I'm seeing."

Richard nodded, reading through the material before he passed it on to Timothy. He thought through what he had read. Nollan was right. Something was off here. Neither one of the men know what but they were determined to find it out.

"Nollan? This comment that you made. About the product?" Silver raised her head even as Sorley continued to read. She knew that Sorley was making notes and would do a financial investigation on the company and the product.

"The product? Yes. It is dangerous as it is. It is a new product, not yet manufactured. If we stop it now and they make the corrections that are needed, it will be fine. But I'm not sure that they will."

Tate looked at Richard and then at Nollan.

"This company? Did you know that it has been involved in a lawsuit a few years ago? They settled out of court so the terms are sealed."

Richard had turned to her as she was speaking. Sorley was nodding. He had heard the same about the company.

"I'll start a search, Richard. Nollan, can you give me whatever information that you have? Then I'll make it a priority."

"Emma's involved?" Silver nodded as she looked at Naomi. "Of course, she is. Abe hasn't threatened to put you away somewhere yet?"

The team laughed, leaving Nollan to stare at them.

"Abe is a friend. He has a security team that does training as well. He would hide us somewhere if Richard asked." Naomi simply wrapped an arm around him, his own arm wrapping around her.

"That he would." Richard studied the couple before he continued. "This is where it does get dangerous, you two. Naomi, you're familiar with what we do now. Nollan, we work as we can to find out who it is. We try and protect you as much as we can. We just ask that you be as alert as you can be. Now, how be we spend some time in prayer? We are going to need that. Naomi, Nollan, you are prayed for by many people. Naomi, you are familiar with that. Nollan, I am not sure how your church works. This is how ours does. We don't need a lot of information. Other than you two need prayer."

"Thank you, Richard. It's not quite how our church works. Some of the people do demand information that they don't require. I was always reluctant to ask for prayer because of that."

"You don't have to worry about that here." Timothy spoke up. "If you need to talk with someone, try Silas. He and Madigan went through some pretty rough stuff. They had one of those adventures. He'll talk with you. Nothing you say to him is written down or passed on to anyone. The only one that he would speak to would be Madigan and only if you had agreed to that."

"I see. I'll keep him in mind." Nollan paced the area, his thoughts far away. His frown was intense, causing the others to look at him and then at one another.

Naomi finally stepped into his path, stopping him. His hands rested on her shoulders as he stared down at her. He could see the worry and fear in her eyes that she was trying hard to hide.

"Nollan? We're not going to solve this tonight. Not by a long shot. So, how be we sit and then we pray? We need some of Richard's prayers tonight."

———

Nollan nodded, drawing out a chair for her to sit on before he sat beside her. He didn't see the speculative glances sent their way.

"Richard? I'm told that we need your prayers. Would you?"

Richard simply nodded, bowed his head, and prayed. Nollan said afterwards that he felt as if he had been taken right to God's throne. Naomi assured him that was how Richard's prayers worked.

Chapter 29

Nollan stood staring down at the findings on his computer monitor a week later. He raised his head. This was what he had expected to find, he knew. He was satisfied with it. Finishing his report, he sent it off to the CEO of the company.

He was done his work for the week, even though it was only Thursday. He needed to get away for a day. Heading for his car, Nollan simply drove out of town, heading for his aunt's home.

Maggie turned as she heard Nollan's voice, surprised to see him. She hugged him and then shoved him into a chair. She sat, her hands reaching for his, a position that was common to them. This was how she reached out to him. Maggie's prayer reached his ears.

"Nollan? I'm surprised to see you. You weren't due to come for another week." Maggie studied her nephew, seeing the changes in his face and also the stress. "Talk to me."

Nollan drew in a deep breath, knowing that his aunt would want nothing but all of what he could tell her. And he needed her counsel and her prayers. He poured out everything that he could that had happened in the last few weeks. Maggie listened, her eyes not moving for his face. She sighed. She knew that it had been bad, whatever it was that he was facing. Maggie had not just expected it to be this bad.

Her head bowed one more time as she prayed for him. Nollan swiped at his shoulder to dry the tears that were falling. He didn't hear his uncle enter but Jake watched him before he handed him a handkerchief, sitting beside him and then raising his own voice in prayer.

Jake had been in the hallway as Nollan had begun to speak, not wanting to intrude. He felt that he finally had to.

Nollan's head was raised, a thank you uttered to his aunt and uncle. Jake turned keen eyes on Nollan, sensing that Nollan was restless.

"Nollan? How happy are you in your work?" Jake's question shook Nollan, even as it had surprised him.

Nollan knew that Jake had gone right to the heart of the matter. He was not happy with his work. He didn't enjoy it any more. And that disturbed him. It was supposed to be the work that he stayed in until he retired. Now, he could feel God nudging him into a different direction. He just wasn't sure what that direction was.

"Uncle Jake, I'm not. The last month has been hard. I don't enjoy it. Is that even possible?" He turned to Jake, seeking his advice. Nollan knew that his uncle would be praying even as he answered him.

"It is entirely possible, Jake. We make decisions as young people that sometimes aren't where we are to be. That is how life works. Now, we can either stay in that work and be unhappy and stagnate. Or we can seek God's direction and move to where He wants us. This can be stressful and somewhat fearful. We are praying for you, Nollan. We have sensed this uncertainty in you that is unusual. You are usually certain of what you want and go for it."

"I do. It's just that I don't know who is after me. We've talked, Uncle Jake, about what has happened. The police have no idea who it is. Naomi is in danger as well. I want to keep her safe. But I don't have that right. Not yet."

"Not yet? That tells me that your heart is involved, son. You have never shown any interest in any other young lady. Yet, you do in Naomi. God placed you in Maggie's tea room that day. Who knows where Naomi would be now if you had not stepped in? I won't ask where you're heading with her. You'll tell us when you are able to. But I sense that there is a connection between you two that God has allowed. Pray about it, son. Listen to counsel given by us and your friends. But most importantly, listen to God. He will direct you to where you need to be.

"Now, what can we do to help solve this mystery?" Jake was serious about this. He taught in the local college, police investigation in fact.

"I don't know, Uncle Jake. I have information with me that we can go over. I should head for home."

Maggie rested her hand on Nollan's head.

"Not tonight, Nollan. Tonight, you stay here. Then head home tomorrow. Let your lady know that you are safe. If you don't, she may end up at your place. And we don't want that."

Nollan nodded, rising to his feet, heading for the living room. He sent off a quick text to Naomi, muted his phone and then walked out of the back door. He roamed the yard that he had spent many an hour mowing the grass before he turned to stare at the home. His childhood home had been sold when his parents died. He had no interest in keeping it. Now, he wasn't sure that he had made the right decision. He was second guessing himself a lot, he knew. And that was not his character.

Naomi frowned as she read the text message that Nollan had sent. She sighed. So much for tonight. She had have thought of showing up at his place with a meal. That was out. Instead, she reached for a bottle of water and headed for her office. Naomi planned to work on their mystery for a while. At least that had been her plan. A call from Nikki sidetracked her to the living room. Nikki had been burdened about her sister and had called, just to talk. Much laughter was scattered throughout their conversation.

Rising at last, Naomi shot a glance at the clock. It was almost bedtime and she had not done the research that she had planned to do. She had shrugged. She had really needed a night off. Nikki had seen to that. She retired, her sleep dreamless. Naomi did not hear the sounds outside her home. Her security system picked up the movement of the men who sought to gain entry to her home.

Richard drove home thoughtfully. He had been at a meeting with the church committee that he was part of and was heading home. His thoughts turned to Naomi and Nollan. He was just not sure how to proceed with what they had. There was one piece of information that was missing. He knew that if they

———

155

could find it, they could solve the mystery. Emma had been in touch. She simply stated that she was forwarding information to them all. She just asked that they read it and then call her.

Chapter 30

Nollan headed for home the next morning, feeling much better. His uncle's counsel the night before had resonated with him. It was the type of counsel that his father would have given. He appreciated it. Nollan also knew that he did not need to take it but he likely would.

Turning into his driveway, he slowed and came to a stop. He sat for a moment, staring at his house. He felt as if he was at a crossroads and wasn't sure which way to turn. He walked at last towards his home, not paying attention to his surroundings.

Running footsteps startled Nollan. As he spun around, he was hit soundly and taken to the ground. Stunned, he was unable to avoid the blows that hammered at him. His assailant rose, pulling off his gloves and then walking away. He didn't look back at the body on the ground.

Late that afternoon, Naomi pulled her vehicle in beside Nollan's. She had come looking for him. He had not answered her text message from that morning when she had responded to him. That was very unusual for him. She stood by her car, a frown on her face. She felt uneasy, not sure why. Walking around Nollan's car, her steps halted abruptly before she was running towards the lawn. Dropping to her knees, Naomi reached to assess him, feeling for a pulse. Relief flooded through her. He was alive. Her phone was out as she called for emergency help.

Standing back as the paramedics worked on Nollan, Naomi simply shook her head. She couldn't say much as she didn't know what had happened or when it had. She had just come to look for her and found him like that.

Bill was back from his vacation and was the detective called out. He shook his head before he walked towards Naomi.

"Naomi? What's going on?"

Naomi shrugged, not sure herself.

"I don't know, Bill. I found him like this. He's been beaten."

"That's what I was told. Head off after him, Naomi. I'll call his family."

Bill watched as she walked or almost ran to her vehicle and took off after the paramedic rig. His phone out, he made the call to Maggie. Rubbing his finger across the phone screen, he made another decision. It was time, he decided, that these two were put into protective custody. Naomi would fight him on that, he knew

"Richard? Yeah, I'm back. What are you up to tonight? You're free? I'm at Nollan's. He's been beaten. Naomi found him. We have no idea at this time how long it has been. I've sent her off after him."

Richard sighed. He had been expecting a call like this.

"I'll head that way. I hear what you're not saying. She'll fight us on this, you do know that."

Bill gave a bark of laughter before he sobered.

"I do know that. Call me when you get your plans made. Don is available, he tells me, if you need help. Your people can't do it at night."

"No, they can't. I won't ask that of them. I'll coordinate with Don." Richard pocketed his phone before his head bowed and he prayed for his team mate and her fellow.

Naomi turned as she felt an arm across her shoulder. Richard was there. She was glad of that. She could use his support and also his prayers.

"How is he, Naomi?" Richard's voice was quiet.

"I'm not sure. Michael is here and has gone back to see. Apparently he has been staying with Nollan off and on." Naomi shoved at the hair brushing at her face. "Nollan was at his aunt's last night. He should have gotten home around nine, Michael thinks. He wasn't working today." She didn't say anything. She didn't have to.

Richard's eyes closed before he spoke.

"What time did you find him?"

"It was after four. He's been laying there all that time. Who knows how that harmed him."

"They'll take that into account as they treat him. There was no rain and the day was warm." Richard sat beside Naomi, praying for his friend and her guy. He didn't need to say anything. Naomi could read him to a certain extent and would know that he was praying for her.

"Richard? How do we do this? How do we stay safe? I don't want to go into hiding. It never solves anything. In fact, it delays the inevitable."

"It does. We may need to stick you away somewhere just until we can get some plans made. Don is around and told Bill that he was available if we need him. I intend to reach out to Abe as well and see what he can suggest."

"Thank you, Richard. I don't want to do that with Don unless we don't have any other option. I have lined up some safe houses for him that we can use. He asked me to do that today. He said that you had agreed with that."

"I did. I know that he does that himself. There must be a reason that he's reached out to you."

"There is. He thinks someone is following his team too closely for them to use their own safe houses."

"That could be very true." Richard's eyes closed as he prayed. He was exhausted that day. This with his team had disturbed his sleep.

"Richard? What if we're right about someone being after you? Could that explain part of it?" Naomi waited for him to respond, knowing that he would think it through before he did so.

"We've felt that all along, haven't we? It's entirely possible. But someone is after you or is after Nollan. Did you two ever connect before that day?"

"Not that I know of. I went to college in Oak City. He went elsewhere." She turned as she heard a sound. "Michael?"

"Did you take police investigations as part of your course?" Michael waited for her response.

"I did. Why?" Naomi was puzzled at his question.

"Because you would have had my dad as your teacher."

Naomi stared at him, her mind working.

"That's our connection. Your father. Now, we need to look into that." She sighed, exhaustion causing her to slump in her seat.

"And we will." Richard sent of a text to Bill before he turned back to Michael. "Michael, we'll need to speak with your father."

"And you can. He and Mom are on their way here." Michael rose and walked away, heading for his parents. "Dad? We found the connection that we were talking about."

"You have? And that would be?" Jake watched his son, seeing the agitation in him.

"We did. Your course on police investigation that you teach. Naomi took it."

Jake's keen eyes focused on Naomi. He remembered her after all the years. She had been one that had stood at the top of her class, a better student than he had ever taught.

"I remember her." Jake walked towards Naomi. He stopped in front of her.

Richard had stood up as Jake had approached. He didn't know this man, but he seems to know Naomi.

"Naomi? I didn't realize that it was you that Nollan was speaking about." Jake reached out to hug her. "I often wondered what happened to my star student."

Naomi remembered to snap her mouth closed before she returned the hug.

"And my favourite professor. Have you heard how Nollan is?" That was Naomi's only concern.

Chapter 31

Maggie stood at Nollan's bedside that night. She was worried about him. The physician had been around, talking with them. He was concerned, he agreed, that Nollan had not awakened fully, even though he was starting to rouse. Michael and Jake had left, not being able to absent themselves from their work.

Naomi paused in the doorway, not sure if she should enter. Her feet took her forward, finding Maggie's arm out to draw her to her side.

"He's starting to rouse, Naomi. The physician has said that he should be awake by morning." Maggie watched Naomi closely.

"That's good. You're staying overnight?"

"I was going to but I was told that visiting hours end soon. I'm not sure what to do. I don't have a vehicle."

"You can stay with me. I'll bring you back in the morning." Naomi touched Nollan's face and then walked away, finding a seat in the waiting room.

Maggie watched her walk away and then sighed. She began to pray for her.

The next morning, Nollan had roused. He glared at Bill as Bill stared back at him.

"I don't remember anything, Bill. I know that I stayed at my aunt's the night before. I don't remember driving home. None of your questions are going to make that happen."

Bill grinned at him briefly.

"That's okay, Nollan. It is what it is. You may remember. You may not. The assault was not caught on your security cameras. That was planned."

"I gathered that. I have no idea who it was." Nollan's eyes closed for a moment. He knew that his aunt had been there and then left, a friend appearing to drive her to the tea room.

"Michael found a connection between you two."

"He did? What is it?"

"Your uncle. We have never connected Naomi's college with your family. Apparently, he taught one of her courses."

"Police investigation. Of course." Nollan's head went back on the pillow. "I should have made that connection."

"No, not really. We should have asked though. I have someone tracking back through our investigation to see how that was missed."

"I see." Nollan sat up, grimacing with pain. He had not broken any bones. The beating had left him with soft tissue injuries and bruising. That would take time to heal, he knew. He was just impatient to have it over with.

"Listen, if you need a lift home, I'm free. I'm off duty as of now. And I know that your discharge papers are ready."

"That would be great, Bill. I appreciate it." Nollan watched Bill walk away before he dressed and headed after him, his steps slow as pain throbbed through his body.

Naomi stared at him that night. She wasn't prepared for the bruises colouring his face, hidden as they were by the growth of beard. Nollan had not been able to handle the pain of shaving. He had decided finally to shave off his beard.

"Nollan, are you sure that you should be home?"

"I am, my love. I am. Come here." He reached to hug her, not letting go of her as she struggled for a moment. "I'm fine, Naomi. I've been hurt. Yes, it was hours before I was found. God was there, my love. He protected me even then."

Naomi's head was against his chest. She could hear his heart beating strong and steady.

"I know, Nollan. I know. It's just that I was so scared when I saw you. I thought that you were dead."

"They tried and failed." He turned them towards his office. "I've been working on something. Uncle Jake talked to me the other night. He picked up that I'm not happy with my work. He's so right in that."

"You're not." Naomi simply agreed with him. "It's obvious that you're not. What would you like to do?"

Nollan shrugged, not sure how to respond.

"I really don't know. I need to seek counsel on that. I would covet your prayers as well." He seated her on the loveseat before he reached for a folder. "This is what I'm thinking."

She took the folder, knowing that when she looked inside at what he had done, it might well change their relationship. She was not prepared for that. Her heart lifting in prayer, Naomi opened the folder, reading through his notes. She paused, looking up at him, a frown on her face.

"You're sure about this?"

"I am. I have asked before to teach. I also just set it to one side. This is a well-known college. I would be doing online courses. I think that I could do this."

"I'm sure that you can. Okay, so we pray this over. Why would you think it would change what we are?"

Nollan reached for her once more, the folder dropped to the floor.

"I am in love with you, Naomi, and have been for a while. I don't want to lose you. We still need to get through whatever it is that we are involved in. I don't want to see that end our friendship."

"That won't happen." Naomi hugged him. "I love you too. People have been picking up on this, you know." She smirked as he grinned at her.

"They have been, haven't they? We have very smart friends and families." He reached to kiss her before he sat back, staring into the distance.

"Nollan?" Naomi had to speak his name again before he looked at her. "What did you just think of?"

"I think I know who it is. And if it's that man, we are in more danger than we thought." Nollan felt more fear in him for his lady than he had felt. He just didn't know how to keep her safe.

"Nollan? Who? Who is it that you suspect?" Naomi could barely get out the words.

Nollan looked at her once more, uttering the name. He saw her understanding and then her fear.

Chapter 32

Two days later, Nollan stood in his office. He didn't want to be there. Not any more, he decided. It was a Saturday. He wasn't usually in on a Saturday. Naomi roamed the office, on guard. She knew that this was coming to a head and that they would face the ones responsible.

Nollan's head turned slightly as he heard Naomi's soft footsteps. He grimaced with pain, his movement restricted. He had stared at his face in the mirror that morning, a hand touching it. He had finally shaved, the pain intense at times. Naomi had stared at him as he had stood in her entryway a while after that and just shaken her head.

Naomi assessed the building once more. It was not the first time that this had been done. She was afraid for Nollan. The beating two days ago had shaken both of them. She didn't know if she could handle him being hurt again. She didn't know that Nollan's thoughts were the same as his.

Pulling out her phone, Naomi scrolled through her messages, responding to the ones that she needed to. Richard had sent one early that morning, just asking that they stay safe that day. She had smiled and then responded. Her phone was back in her pocket.

Nollan came to find her, reaching for her hand as he locked the door behind him. Once in his truck, he headed for Ev's diner, determined to put aside how he was feeling and just enjoy the day with his lady. He didn't see the looks that he received as they entered before the patrons nodded. His assault had made the newspaper, and most of those present had read about it.

Andrew watched Nollan and Naomi enter, his thoughts troubled for a moment. His daughter patted at his arm and drew his attention her way, a huge smile covering his face. The little girl was the delight of their lives, he knew.

"He's hurting, Andrew." Phoebe's voice was low, loud enough that only Andrew heard her.

"He is. Naomi is as well. They're a couple, whether they will acknowledge that yet or not."

Phoebe studied them and nodded. Andrew was correct. They were a couple. Coming out into the community as they were? That showed the world that they were dating. Anyone who knew Naomi knew that she didn't date. Yet, here she was with Nollan.

Nollan watched his lady, seeing that she had not relaxed. She was in work mode, he decided and then sighed. This was how it was to date her. He reached for her hand, his warm on hers,

"Naomi? You're troubled." He waited patiently for her to respond.

Naomi shook the fog off that she as if she was under. Her smile lighted her face.

"I am, Nollan. This isn't fair to you, to be like this." Her words paused as his hand tightened on hers. "You're okay with this?"

"I am, Naomi. Being protective and hyper-aware of where you are and who is around you is part of you.

I would not trade it. I love that about you. You care about whoever it is that you are with.”

Naomi slowly digested his words. *He was correct,* she thought. *That's how God made me. Thank you, Lord, for all my gifts and talents, even the ones that I wish that I didn't have.*

“Thank you, Nollan. There are not many people out there who recognize that. I have had friends desert me because of this. I can't change who I am.”

His smile warmed her heart.

“I would not change one thing about you. And that is a fact.” He looked up as the server approached to take their orders. “Thank you.” He turned back to her, finding instead that she was studying the patrons in the diner. “Naomi?”

“Someone is in here, Nollan. I can't tell who. They're all townsfolk.”

“I assumed that. Now, what are the plans for the day?” He grinned as she shook a finger at him.

“Plans? For the day? As in you and me together all day?” She smirked at him.

“Yes, exactly that. My dream is that we spend every day together.” His eyes raised as he felt watched, taking his thoughts from Naomi.

Naomi watched him and sighed. *This is going so well,* she thought. *Someone is watching us from in here. Lord, this is when we need Your protection. I mean, I know that you allow things to happen. I just wish that this was over. I hate feeling tracked and trapped.*

Rising at last, Naomi headed for the exit, stepping out into sunshine and warmth. The summer was drawing to a close. She didn't want it to end but seasons came and went. She was reminded of the verses that described how there was a season to everything.

Nollan pointed to his truck, heading that way. He tucked her inside and then headed for his seat. He paused as he inserted the key into the ignition. He felt very uneasy that day, expecting that something would happen. He disliked that feeling.

Richard stood outside the diner, watching as Nollan left. He was worried about Naomi. He just didn't know who was after her. That concerned him. Shaking his head, he headed into the diner, waving at those he knew. Avery was waiting, waving him through to his mother's office.

"Richard? You're worried?" Avery went right to the point.

"I am. This bit with Naomi has been almost too much for my team." Richard sat in one of the upholstered chairs in the sitting area that Ev had designed in her office.

"I am sure that it is. I know Andrew is very concerned about that. What can I do?"

"What can you do? That's a good question. I'm not sure."

"Tell me everything that you can. Names. Places. Thoughts. Whatever." Avery reached for a pad of paper and began to write.

Richard did just that. He laid it all out for Avery. He sat back, drained. His head dropped as he prayed for Naomi and Nollan, and yes, the rest of his team.

Ev approached the men, a tray of food handed to Avery. He was on his feet, moving after his mother.

"Mom, what have you heard?"

"About Naomi? Not a lot. There have been very few rumours coming out about what she is facing. Old George would be someone to speak with, though, if you can find him."

Avery nodded, turning to face the office.

"I will try. And I'll mention that to Richard as well. He's puzzled, Mom. He just can't put a finger on who or why."

"No? Then, let me think about it. Naomi is in here a lot, sometimes on her own. She doesn't say much about her work or her past. She is more interested in whoever it is that she is speaking with."

"That sums her up so well." Avery returned to the office, finding Richard scribbling madly on a pad of paper. "Richard? You thought of something?"

"I did. I just pray that I'm wrong. Somehow, I don't think that I am. And Nollan and Naomi are off somewhere today. I pray that they're safe. Naomi has muted her phone, I think. She's not answering."

Avery was deeply concerned. He reached for Richard's note, his face growing stern as he read through them.

"You're sure about this?" He had no doubt that Richard was.

"I am. So help me, I am. And my team has scattered today. I won't call them back. They need this time as couples." Richard rose to pace

"This makes it hard, Richard. I know that Bill is on duty today. Andrew was around with Phoebe and their little one."

"No, just us for now. You're working here, though."

"Not really. I came just to spend time with Mom. She's fine if I leave. Come on, my friend. On your feet. Where do you want to go?"

"My place. I have the programs there that I need to search." Richard reached for his phone to read the email that had just come through. "Bless her. Emma is on the same track. She's forwarding information to me and to Bill as well."

Chapter 33

Her senses tingling, Naomi spun in a circle. *This was probably not that good an idea,* she decided, *to come here for a walk. We're in danger. How do we get out of here?* She reached for Nollan's hand, a finger to her lips to shush him as she tugged him with her.

Her hand tight in his, Nollan ran with Naomi, the jarring of his feet hitting the path jarring his body. He could feel the pain intensifying. That was not what he wanted to feel, he decided.

"Where to?" Nollan's voice was very quiet. He studied his lady, seeing her attention was not on him but on her surroundings. He realized that she was in work mode.

Naomi scanned the area, her sense alert. She could feel the evil stalking them, chasing them through the park and along the paths. This is not what they need. She spun for a moment, Nollan's hand dropping from hers. She reached for his hand again, heading away from town and towards the edge of the park. This was a park where she walked or ran frequently. It had become as familiar as her own backyard.

Heading for a deeply-treed area, Naomi paused, struggling to control her breathing. Nollan leant against a tree, his breathing ragged. Pain was evident on his face. Naomi felt bad about that but knew there wasn't anything that she could too about that. She listened, her senses alert. There were footsteps along the paths and angry voices cursing. Her eyes slid closed. Naomi had managed to get them to safety for now, but it was far from over.

Her phone out, she sent a quick text off to Richard, asking him to meet them. He would, she knew, if he was able to. That was not a concern. She just had to make sure that they were safe until then.

Nollan's mouth opened to speak before he snapped it closed. *No,* he thought, *I can't interrupt her. She's turned protective of me. I have to let her do this. She'll do everything to protect both of us. I just never expected to see her drop into work mode so quickly. Lord, You have promised to protect us. Please, Lord, spare my lady. Protect her. Guide her as she works to find somewhere safe for us to hide. I am sure that her friends will come to help. Only, I don't know that they will have time. I am claiming Your promises, dear Lord.*

Naomi pointed away from the trail, moving quickly along a narrow path, the trees and shrubs brushing at them. Nollan wasn't sure how she even knew where she was or where to go. He certainly didn't. But then, he had not made it a habit to explore remote areas of the parks. He knew that Naomi likely did, just given her line of work.

"Naomi?" Nollan pulled her to a stop. His voice was very low as he spoke.

"What?" Naomi snapped at him and then sighed. "I'm sorry. This is not your fault. We need to find somewhere to hide. I'm just not sure where."

"I know that. I just don't know where." Nollan searched the area, knowing full well that he had no idea what he was looking for.

"I need to find a place to stick you away. I'm not sure any more which of us that they're after."

"Nor do I." Nollan grew quiet, letting her work. He didn't want to disturb her train of thought and put them into more danger.

Richard reached for his phone. It had been chiming on and off for the last hour. He had ignored it as he and Avery worked through the programs and their search. He grew stern as he read Naomi's text.

"Naomi's in trouble, Avery. She's being chased in Old Mill Park." Richard was on his feet, heading for the door, Avery on his heels.

"Did she say why?" Avery fastened his seatbelt as Richard took off at a higher rate of speed than was normal for him.

"Just that they were being chased. She's near the mill from what she said." Richard's mind was working. "How do we do this, Avery? She's not going to be out in plain sight. And if I show up, they'll know where she is."

"Then, I go in. I walk that park when I can. I spend a lot of time near the old mill." Avery's mind was racing as was Richard's, trying to come up with a plan and just not doing that.

Naomi headed for the old mill, hoping against hope that Richard would arrive. It would just depend, she knew, on where he was and what he was up to. She paused for a moment before she ran quickly across the open area, disappearing into the mill, Nollan right behind her. Naomi hesitated for a moment before she headed for the second floor. There were places there that they could hide. She and Silver had found them one day, surprise on their faces as they did so.

Nollan followed, uncertainty in his mind as he did so. He had explored the mill a couple of times. He just didn't know where Naomi was heading, but she seemed to have a destination in mind.

Naomi reached for a wall, shoving at a spot. Nollan stood in amazement as the wall move slightly, enough to let them into a room. Naomi closed the wall, pacing the small room after she did so. There was light from a hole in the wall. Nollan inspected it closely, realizing that it had been a window at one point. Naomi shook her head at him as his mouth opened.

Leaning close to his ear, Naomi cautioned him about speaking. He nodded, reaching for his phone and muting it. They didn't need it ringing. They could hear noise on the other side of the wall, indicating that the men had somehow decided that was where they were hiding. The cursing and voices continued to rise as the men's anger heightened.

Nollan wrapped Naomi in a hug, feeing her hugging him back. They were trapped for now, he knew. Just how and when they would be able to leave was uncertain.

Richard paused as he neared the mill. They had walked in as rapidly as they could, both men on alert. They listened to the angry voices. Richard was relieved. At least, Naomi and Nollan were safe for now, he thought.

Avery pointed towards the door. Richard nodded, moving that way. They stepped inside, careful not to step on any debris or hit it and knock it out of the way. They listened as the men stormed down the stairs, separating to stand on either side of the broken stairway. Richard took his man down quickly, the man's belt used to bind his hands. He looked up to see Avery had done the same. Richard pointed to the stairs, Avery nodding as he pulled out his phone. If he was not mistaken, these two men were wanted by multiple police forces across the country.

Richard searched for Naomi, not finding her. That worried him. He didn't think that they had been abducted. His phone was out as he sent a quick text message to her. Hearing a sound behind him, he spun, staring as a wall moved and Naomi and Nollan appeared. He walked over to look into the room and then nodded as Naomi shut it.

"We have the two men. Avery and I were working on something when you sent that text. Stay here for now. Avery had called it in." Richard walked to the top of the stairs, watching as the officers streamed in and took the men away. Bill was there, he saw, before he walked down the stairs.

"Bill? I didn't expect to see you here."

Bill nodded, reading Richard's face. *He knows where Naomi and Nollan are and isn't prepared to tell me,* he thought. *Okay, we'll play that game for now.*

Chapter 34

Naomi waited quietly, her hand on Nollan's arm keeping him in place. She knew that Bill was there as were other officers. Richard wanted them to stay where they were for a reason. She shook her head at Nollan as he pointed towards the stairs. Richard had picked up on something, Naomi knew. Staying where they were and staying quiet might be the only way that they survived. She had been in that very position too many times to not stay still.

Richard moved away from Bill. He didn't want Bill heading up the stairs. And he would do that, Richard knew, if he didn't get them out of there.

"Richard? Where are they?" Bill waited for Richard to speak. He sighed as Richard walked out of the mill, Avery beside him. "Come on, Richard. Talk to me. Where are Naomi and Nollan?"

"For now, they're safe. As of today, I'm putting them into protective custody. Don's sending a couple of men to help in the overnight hours. We'll keep in touch, Bill."

Bill was frustrated. He had been handed information that he needed to verify with Naomi and Nollan. Only that didn't seem as if it would happen.

"Richard, I need to talk with them. I have information to go over with them." Bill stood almost toe to toe with Richard, leaving Avery slightly amused as to who would win.

"And we'll be in touch. For now, they're in hiding." Richard was adamant about that. He would not tell Bill that the couple was upstairs in the mill. He couldn't do that. He trusted Naomi to flee with Nollan if it came to that and then contact him.

Bill walked away at last, knowing that Richard would not tell him where the couple was. He knew that without Richard saying anything.

Avery waited Richard to speak. Richard turned at last, moving through the mill, Avery going the same.

"Okay, Richard. Where do we take them?" Avery waited for his friend to speak.

"For now, we head to my place. We'll decide from there where to go. With three of my team married, they'll want to be at home at night. That means they go back and forth from the office."

"You have a good tight set-up there, Richard. You can stash them there for now. And know that Don is around."

"He is. We talked last night, coming up with a plan. I just didn't expect it to happen so soon."

"None of us ever do. Now, let's head off with them."

Richard nodded, not quite comfortable with that.

"Avery, I'll take them with me. I'll grab Nollan's keys. Can you drop off his truck at his home? I'll follow and let him grab what he needs for a week or so."

———

"A week or so? You're not expecting it to last much longer than that." Avery was reading Richard correctly.

"No, to tell you the truth, I'm not. I know that Bill is not near the conclusion of his investigation. This is starting to move and move rapidly. This is where it always gets dangerous for our protectees."

"And it's always worse when it's one of your own. I get that. Let's move. I don't like the feeling that I'm getting." Avery headed away, Richard having retrieved Nollan's keys.

"All right, Nollan. Let's move. We'll stop by your house to grab some clothes and whatever it is that you will need for the next week. Naomi, you know the drill."

Naomi nodded, knowing that Richard was taking them some place. And that she didn't want to do.

"I do, unfortunately. I'll need to grab my bag."

"And we will. For now, you'll be at my place. If we need to, you'll have to find us somewhere else. Don is sending in a couple of his men for the overnight hours."

Naomi nodded, having already come to that conclusion. Her head leant against the truck window. She didn't want to do this but she had no choice. She turned to watch Nollan, finding a sad look on his face. He was quiet, too quiet, she decided.

Richard and Naomi paced around the outside of Nollan's house as he ran in to quickly pack a bag and then grab what he needed for work. He stood for a moment, looking around his house, not sure when he would be back. He just prayed that he would be. He reached for his well-worn Bible and dropped it into his briefcase before he grabbed his bags and headed for the door.

Richard nodded at Naomi as she reached for the door handle. He knew that she would be very quick, grabbing her already packed bag and whatever else it was that she needed. He didn't like to do this. Unfortunately, they had no choice.

Naomi's eyes were in constant motion as Richard drove towards his home. They were followed, she knew. That was all part and parcel of what they faced. It had been a blessing, she knew that they no longer had to do it for clients. That she did not miss, not one bit.

Nollan had no words. He was still in shock, having had to run for his life once more and then just being told to pack what he needed. His freedom had walked away from him for now. He didn't like that.

"Richard? Where are we heading?" Nollan frowned as he watched Richard drive in a seemingly endless manner.

"To my place. We'll hole up there for now. My team is with us during the day. They will continue to train, other than for Naomi. She stays hidden. A friend is sending in team members for the overnight hours. We'll see how it comes from there. If we have to move to a safe house, Naomi will have some in place for us. We may need to move suddenly. Be prepared for that."

Richard's voice seemed harsh but that was worry doing that.

Naomi shot Nollan a compassionate look. This was all new to him. All she could do right at the moment was pray for him and for herself. Even as she was in work mode, her mind was searching through the verses that she had memorized, seeking for the reassurance of God's protection for them and for her team.

Chapter 35

Three days later, Nollan shoved away from the desk where he had been working. He was confused, to say the least. The company whose information he has passed on to Bill had suddenly shut down. He could find no reason for that. And another company that had contacted him had shown similar results to the first one. Nollan had reached out to Emma, asking what her thoughts were.

Emma's email that morning had concerned him, to put it mildly. He had not expected the results that she had found. He now had to decide what to do about that. Nollan had forwarded his work on to Bill, asking that he verify it.

Naomi looked up from where she was working, a frown on her face that smoothed away. She was used to this, she knew, but Nollan wasn't. On her feet, Naomi approached Nollan.

"Nollan? You look worried?"

Nollan nodded as he turned towards her.

"I am. I don't like what I am finding here. And I have reached out to both Bill and Emma. They're working on more information for me." He reached to wrap her into a hug, not sure if he should be doing that when she was working. "Another company has the same appearance as the first one. And the first company has closed up."

"That's strange. They usually don't just do that, do they?" Naomi stared at him, her thoughts racing as to why that would be.

"No, they don't. Not unless they go bankrupt. Even then, there is a process that they go through. I have not seen this before."

"I see. Nollan, come. It's lunchtime. Let's eat. Richard and the others will be in soon. I offered to make their lunch. You can help."

Nollan grinned at her, following her to Richard's kitchen. They worked away in silence, broken only by the occasional whistle that Nollan uttered.

Richard entered, his glance on them, hearing the conversation of the other three behind him. The trainees had left, their training done. He was glad to be done with that aspect of his week. Now, it only remained to keep Nollan and Naomi safe. How they were to do that, he wasn't sure. He could see both of them getting restless under the restraints. Nollan was more ready to break loose, he knew. He also knew that Naomi would be right behind him. And that could mean their death.

Naomi's conversation and fun with her friends and team mates helped to ease the guilt that Nollan felt. He excused himself near the end of the meal, needing to find a place where he could pray. He felt the danger building around them. He didn't know how to stay safe.

Timothy was on his feet, shadowing Nollan until he saw the other man sitting. He chose a chair near him to sit and watch. His own prayers were wafting to heaven. He knew that they would be answered. It was the answer that concerned him. They might not like that answer. He acknowledged that and that God did have a plan for their lives.

Nollan raised his head at last, feeling refreshed and renewed. He was not surprised to find Timothy near him. It was what he had come to expect.

"Timothy? How do we do this? We can't stay hidden forever." Nollan leaned forward, his chin resting on his closed fist, an elbow on the chair arm.

"No, you can't. No one can. We're working through some plans. We are not at a point where we could use your input." Timothy was hesitant about that. He really didn't know Nollan well enough to judge what he would suggest.

"I see. And you're not sure if I will have the input that you need. I will. I want this over. I have plans for my life that I want to move forward with. God is leading me into something different. I need to be free to do that."

"Enforced quiet. That's what this is. You either use it to improve yourself and your walk with God or you fight it and lose. You're a fighter, Nollan. You suit Naomi and she suits you." Timothy was on his feet, walking away, leaving Nollan staring after him before nodding.

He's right, isn't he, Lord? We do suit one another. Protect my lady, please, dear Lord.

Nollan walked the other way, heading for his laptop. He had work to do that he could not put off.

———

Lost in his work, he didn't see Naomi approaching him and then sitting nearby, her attention on him. He roused at last, a frown on his face. He needed to be in his office. There were documents there that he needed to access.

Naomi watched, a frown on her face.

"Nollan? What are you thinking?"

Naomi's quiet question brought Nollan's face around to her. She saw the garishness of the bruising but even more, she saw the character of the man. He rose to come and sit beside her, wrapping her into a hug. She leant against him, content, she thought.

"Where do you need to go, Nollan?" Naomi roused enough from her dreams to ask him.

"I need to go to my office. I have to work there for a while." He sighed. "And you're going to tell me that won't happen."

"It can. We just need to coordinate it. Do you need to go today?"

"Not necessarily." Nollan grew quiet, not wanting to move but knowing that eventually, they would need to.

Richard paused for a moment before he approached them, to sit facing them.

"Nollan. I heard what you asked. We can make it happen tomorrow. It's Friday and we don't have a team in for training."

"Thank you, Richard. I appreciate that. I think, however, that I would like to move back home. This

———

may be keeping me safe. It doesn't solve it. That's what we're needing to do."

"I know. I also know that you are aware of any risks that you may face. So, we move you home." Richard was on his feet, walking towards the others.

Nollan stared at him and then at Naomi, finding an understanding smile on her face.

"Did he just do that?"

"Do what? Agree to take you home? He did. He's come to the same conclusion. If he hadn't, he wouldn't have agreed. So, how be you pack up your belongings? He'll take you home today. Tomorrow, I'll spend with you at your office. One of the others will likely be around outside."

Nollan hugged her tighter before he rose to his feet, drawing her up as well.

"I guess then it's time to pack." He walked away, leaving Naomi staring after him, more worried than she cared to admit before she took her worries to her heavenly Father.

Chapter 36

Once more seated in his office, Nollan stared at his desk. He had worked away last night after he had returned home, and had in fact worked the entire night. Now, he was here, ready to fight. He had the information that he needed. Bill had been around to his home early that morning, on his way in, and taken the documentation that Nollan had ready.

"You're sure about this, Nollan?" Bill had been flipping through the paperwork as he asked the question.

"I am, Bill. This is a connection between the two companies. And I can see the connection to Naomi. My uncle taught her one of her courses. The CEO of this company was in that class." Nollan tapped at the papers. "He was not a very good student. From what I could find out, his marks had him failing that class. So how did he end up there?"

Bill had raised his head as Nollan spoke, nodding at the thought.

"Blackmail. He bought his way in. I have someone who can do a financial search for me. And it's not connected to Richard's team." Bill studied him closely. "You know that by naming him, it can become much worse for you."

"I know that, Bill." Nollan's hand ran through his hair. "I know. I just want to ensure that Naomi is safe through all this." He waved his hands as Bill laughed. "I know. I know. She can take care of herself. But she'll put here into the line of fire if needed. They all will. I don't want that on my conscience."

"No, you won't. Leave this with me. Emma's been forwarding material as well that I think will go with this."

"That's what she said. I have copies of it as well." Nollan walked Bill to the door, standing on his front porch to watch him drive away. He closed his eyes, breathing deeply of the fresh morning air. It had rained overnight. The scent of the freshly-washed pavement and gravel and ground always brought comfort to him. Being out after a rainstorm with his father was a memory that he still wanted to live in real life but couldn't.

He came back to the present, hearing Naomi speaking. He stepped to his office door, finding her on her phone. She shrugged as he met her eye. He turned back to his desk, still feeling uneasy without knowing why.

Naomi pocketed her phone. She shared the uneasiness. Something was off in the office. Only, she didn't know what. Heading for the outside, she found Stephen.

"Stephen, Nollan's uneasy inside. I don't know why. He hasn't said. I feel the same way." Her eyes were in constant motion.

Stephen nodded, heading that way. They were both armed that day, something that had startled Nollan when he saw it. They had both agreed with

Richard when he told them to be. He also told them that he would be around that day and would have the others dropping by but not on a set schedule.

Naomi began searching on one side of the building. Stephen took the other side, moving around Nollan in his office. Nollan had stood, a frown on his face.

"Stephen? What are you up to?"

"You're uneasy in here. That's enough for us to know that something is off in here. Those feelings have saved our lives on more than one occasion. Now, pack up everything that you need to take out of here. And I mean everything. Paperwork. Computers. Files. Timothy and Richard are here. They'll load up Richard's truck. We're moving you out of this building. That happens today."

Nollan stared at him until Stephen barked at him to get moving. Silver was there to help, finding boxes and then handing everything off to Richard and Timothy. They filled the truck box of Richard's truck and then moved to Timothy's truck to continue loading what Nollan was packing.

Richard watch his team work before he turned to Nollan, seeing him standing still, staring around, a forlorn look on his face. It was hard on him, Richard understood, having to pack up so quickly. Nollan had not been prepared for that.

Stephen moved quickly towards Richard, anger on his face

"Out now, Richard." Stephen's hand was on Nollan's shoulder, shoving him towards the door. He could hear the running footsteps of his team.

Naomi grabbed Nollan's keys, pointing him to the passenger side. Her team had scattered to the two trucks. Dirt seemed to fly behind them as they accelerated quickly from the area. A shuddering blast shook the vehicles, causing them to swerve on the road before the drivers had them righted and the gas pedal to the floor.

Silver's phone was out as she called it in. She turned to stare behind her, watching the thick plume of smoke rise in the air.

"A bomb. Stephen, had you found it?"

Stephen nodded, a grim look on his face.

"I did. It was in a kitchen cabinet. And it was set on a timer. We had barely any time to get out of there. God protected us once more, Silver."

"He did. I don't know that Nollan was expecting something like this."

"No, I don't think that he would have been. Naomi has gone over as many scenarios as she can think of with him. So has Richard. This was expected but we thought it would be at his home."

"I know. His secretary? How deep have we looked at her?" Silver's mind was working determined to figure it all out.

"We've looked at her and her family. There were no alarms there. This changes it though. I wonder if at some point, she let a delivery person in or left for a bit without setting the alarm. Those are possibilities."

"They are for sure." Silver was out of the truck, on the move to search around Nollan's home. If someone had placed a bomb in his office, then they could well have done the same at his home.

Chapter 37

Nollan was in shock. There was just no other way to describe him. He sat, unmoving, his head in his hands. He had not been prepared to be rushed to pack up his office so quickly. He had been on automatic, he thought, as he had done so.

Naomi watched him, compassion on her face. They had moved quickly, ensuring that he had everything from the building that could be moved as rapidly as possible. She didn't think that they had missed anything important. She heard the three men on her team conversing quietly as they unloaded the trucks and stored the boxes in a spare room.

Richard paused at last, a hand resting on Nollan's shoulder for a moment. He had heard from Bill, who had been shocked at the events. After ensuring that all of them were unharmed, Bill had grimly announced that he would be at the crime scene. When he was done there, he would find Nollan. And Nollan would be speaking with him.

Nollan raised his head last, surprised to see a mug of coffee set in front of him on the kitchen table. He had simply sat when he entered his home, unable to do anything.

"Nollan? What can we do for you?" Richard's voice held compassion and just a touch of worry.

"For me? I really don't know, Richard. Did my office building really blow up?" Nollan wrapped his hands around his mug.

"It did, unfortunately, Nollan. Stephen found a bomb in a kitchen cabinet. It was on a timer. If you had been there on your own, you would not have survived."

Nollan shuddered, having come to that conclusion. He looked around as he heard other voices, one that he didn't recognize.

Richard was on his feet, greeting a friend. Abe Finlay had appeared, sent that way by a premonition of danger.

"You're too late, Abe." Naomi had introduced Abe to Nollan. "We just made it out in time from Nollan's office building."

"That's what Timothy told me on the way in." Abe dropped envelopes on the table. "Emma sent this for you and for Bill. I spoke with him. He said that he's on his way."

"He is. He'll want to speak with you, Nollan." Richard was not surprised that Nollan shoved back from the table and then disappeared through the back door. He likely would have done the same himself.

Abe was not surprised either. He had talked with Naomi the night before, just to assess how she was doing and feeling her out about some of the findings that Emma had come up with.

"He'll run, Richard." Abe knew that Nollan had two options. One was to flee. The other was to stand and fight.

"Naomi won't let him. She'll stand shoulder to shoulder with him and fight it out. She's very protective of him just as he is of her."

"Like that, is it? I know that feeling of wanting to run as far as I could and take Emma with me. Together, we faced our nemesis as did all my guys."

"You did. Nollan needs to hear some of those stories. We've told him about our friends here. He knows what happened with my team. He's met our friends here. So he knows. He's afraid for Naomi. He doesn't want to lose her. That's his fear."

"We all can understand that. We need to keep them covered in prayer." Abe walked away at last, greeting Bill as he arrived. He handed over the information that Emma had sent, a grim look on his face as he did so.

Nollan paced his yard, anger in his steps. He had almost been killed that day. He wanted the one responsible. He had no doubt that he was a target and that for some reason, Naomi had been linked to him. He saw Naomi standing in the middle of the yard, a hand on her weapon, her eyes not on him but on their surroundings. Her stance stopped him in his tracks. Nollan knew that she would protect him, even to giving her life. He just didn't want to admit that might happen. He headed back towards the house, his hand reaching for hers as he passed her. She tightened her hand on his, striding rapidly towards the house. Someone was out there. She could sense them. Nollan needed to be undercover and now.

Richard nodded at the look on her face. He spun, heading for the front door, calling for Stephen and Timothy. Silver headed into the house, moving through to lock the doors and the windows.

Nollan stared at the two ladies, not quite sure what was happening. Naomi pointed to a chair, a stern look on her face until he sat. She then moved around the house, from window to door, just as Silver was.

Nollan watched them, certain now that he really was under attack in his own home. His head sank into his hands once more. He was through, he decided. He had enough. He just didn't know where to start.

Bill had watched Richard's team spring into action. His portfolio hit the kitchen table as he pulled out a chair and sat. He waited for Nollan to react. When he didn't, Bill shook his head.

"Nollan? Talk to me."

"About what?" Nollan's voice was muffled.

"About today. About these companies. About what you're feeling right now."

Nollan shrugged, raising his head.

"How am I supposed to feel? Tell me that. I've been threatened, beaten up, chased from my home. My office building has been destroyed. I am having trouble believing in God right now. How does that sound?"

"Sounds about right. Everyone who has been in a similar situation to yours feels like that." Bill prayed for him, his audible words bringing a sense of peace to Nollan that he needed.

Nollan raised his head, his eyes on the two ladies as they continued to monitor outside.

"How safe are the guys out there?"

"About as safe as they can be. They're trained professionals. They know the risks and weigh the risks and their safety. Sure, they can be hurt, but they accept that. They always have."

"I know. I just don't want them hurt because of me." Nollan's voice held a wealth of emotions, some of which he couldn't even describe.

Chapter 38

Richard raised his head from his reading. He set aside his Bible and rose, heading for the door. He stepped back from the door, surprised to see Nollan standing there.

"Nollan? What are you doing here?" He assessed, seeing the heightened stress in the other man

"I needed to talk with you, Richard." He held up a stack of papers he had in his hand. "I need someone else to look this over. I think that I have found someone else to suspect. I don't want to go to Bill until I understand it better."

"Let's take a look at it. The office, I think, Nollan. Head on that way. I have a fresh pot of coffee on the go. I'll bring you a cup." Richard squinted at the clock. Sandwiches would be a welcome addition to that, he decided.

Nollan looked up as Richard set a tray down near him. He was grateful for that. He had not even thought of food.

Richard waited for Nollan to speak. He reached for the paperwork that Nollan had dropped on the table. He read through it before he looked up at Nollan, to find him sitting with his eyes closed. He could see the fatigue and pain that the other man was feeling.

"Nollan? How do you find this?" Richard tapped at the papers. "I can see this man being responsible for everything. I do know that he is related to the other man who you named."

"He is? I wondered. I didn't have the resources that you do." He sighed. "I have to tell Bill, don't I?"

"At some point. Right now, I would say that this is speculation. We'll look into it for you. This means it is even more dangerous for you."

"And for Naomi as well. I am afraid for her, Richard. Having gone through what I have, I am afraid that he will go after her. And that if he does, she won't survive."

Richard nodded, knowing the character of the man who was named. He turned back to the paperwork, reading through it once more.

"Nollan? This part where you talk about the company? What were they creating?"

"A new type of instrument for taking blood. But it never made sense. It would never have worked. I don't know why they sent it to me."

"A fishing expedition, then. They wanted it to seem that their contact with you was legitimate. Only, it's not. Now, we need to meet with my team." Richard squinted at his watch. "Tomorrow's Saturday. Unfortunately three of them have plans and are out of town. Naomi's around. And my friend Don is around as well. Why don't you just head for the room that you used here and crash? You're almost out on your feet."

Nollan slowly nodded, on his feet to head for the bed. He pulled the covers up over himself, asleep before he could even finish the first sentence of his prayer.

Richard set the paperwork to one side. He would need to read back through it. For now, he simply sent a text to Naomi, asking that she meet at his place in the morning to go over more material that Nollan had found.

He tapped at his chair arm for a moment before he called Don.

"Don? You're around in the morning?"

"I am. What can I do for you?" Don turned from his computer, intent on Richard's call.

"Nollan has found some interesting information on a company that we need to discuss. It's a company that you and I have watched for a couple of years. It's time that we made some plans to take these people down before they kill someone."

"And that is always a possibility with them. I'll be there." Don set aside his phone, his prayers echoing Richard's.

Naomi took the paperwork from Richard the next morning. She had shown up bright and early, needing to know what Nollan had found. She stood and read through it before heading for Richard's office. She made copies, knowing that Richard would not say anything. Naomi stilled as she heard a sound, finding herself trapped by Nollan's arms.

"Nollan? I didn't know that you were here. I mean, I saw your car, so I guess I did." She groaned as he laughed as she groaned.

"Real positive there, sweetheart. Now, what have you discovered?"

"I was about to ask you the same. I know that Don is on his way here. We'll work through it." She hugged him back. "Now, what do we do with you?"

"I have no idea. All I knows that you are important to me. I don't want to see you hurt. That is exactly what I think will happen."

Don studied the couple before nodding. Richard was right. They were a definite couple.

"Nollan? What did you discover about this company?" Don took the sheaf of papers from Richard.

"This company? It's related to the other one that Bill is investigating. And it relates back to someone who was in class with Naomi. That class was taught by my uncle."

"I see." Don found a chair and sat, reading back through the paperwork, making notes as he needed to.

Richard appeared, taking his own copy of the papers. He watched Nollan, finding him looking very troubled.

"Nollan? Talk to us. Tell us what you are thinking."

Nollan nodded, knowing that he had to express himself. Words were not his strong suit. Writing reports were.

"I can try but I'm not good with words. I'm better at writing it down." Nollan felt Naomi's hand on his.

Naomi was on her feet as was Richard. They reached for rolls of paper and taped them to the wall. Don simply handed him a marker and pointed at the paper. Nollan stared at the marker, stared at the three with him, and then at the paper. He began to write, his thoughts moving almost too fast for his hand. He stepped back when he was done, feeling drained. Nolan nodded. He had done what he could. Now it was up to them to sort it out.

Naomi moved along the wall, taking photos of the papers and then forwarded them to her team mates. They would need it, she knew, and would work it as they could. Monday would find them gathering again, after the day of training had finished. And she was certain that Tate, Sorley, and Shanli would be there. She then paused, a thoughtful look on her face, before she forwarded the information to Emma.

Chapter 39

Nollan read back through his notes, a frown on his face. He was missing something or someone. He just didn't know who or what. Naomi was seated beside him, making her own notes.

Richard paused for a moment, a thought crossing his mind. He nodded, knowing that he was on the right track with what Nollan had discovered. He just didn't know if they could find the man at the top and confirm it before something else happened.

"Richard? What do we do now?" Nollan rubbed at his eyes, fatigue draining his ability to think properly.

"Now? We keep searching. Emma's on the track of something. Bill's been given this and has someone working on it. Don's team will work it as well. We'll find the man, Nollan."

"I know that we will at some point. But will it be in time? I don't want Naomi hurt any more than she has been. I've lost so much in property and what not. How much does he want me to lose? And I really don't see the reason for it all."

"Sometimes, the reason is well hidden. We don't know why until the person is arrested and the investigation is completed. I pray that it is over soon for you, Nollan. You need that."

Not one of them heard the sounds of running footsteps that pounded towards the door. The shattering of a window brought Richard and Don to their feet, even as smoke began to fill the office, a smoke that choked them and sent them to the floor.

Naomi was on the move, digging Nollan with her, before he stumbled and went down. Naomi dropped to the floor, crawling towards the door before she found herself picked up. The arms that held her were too much or her to fight against even as she struggled to free her arms. She was carried from the house, her feet kicking at the man carrying her. She was shoved into a vehicle, a hand tight on her wrist. She continued her struggle to escape even as the car sped from the area.

Bill knocked at Richard's door fifteen minutes later. There had been no response to the doorbell. This was not like Richard. A sudden thought had his hand on the doorknob, twisting it. He frowned as the door opened under his hand. He shoved the door open wider, calling for Richard. His hand on his weapon, he moved into the house.

He caught a glimpse of fading smoke and rapidly moved that way. He stopped short as he saw the three bodies, his phone out in an instant to call for help. A shaking hand reached for each man's wrist, a sigh going up as he found their pulses.

Bill managed to maneuver each man to the outside as he waited for help. He hadn't seen Naomi when he knew that she was to be there. This is not what he wanted to find. Not at all.

The responding officers searched the house and then the grounds, not finding a trace of Naomi. Bill was growing increasingly concerned as he stood and listened to a patrol officer. Richard was on his feet, unsteady as he was. Don was sitting up, the oxygen mask still in place. Nollan had been transported to the hospital. He had still not regained consciousness.

"Richard? What happened?" Bill walked towards him, finding Richard looking frantically around, not something that he could remember seeing before.

"Naomi? Do you see her? I don't."

"Naomi's not here. Was she?"

"She was. We were working in the office. The window shattered before we were hit with that gas or smoke or whatever it was. I don't remember much after that."

Bill nodded. It was about what he had expected.

"We need to speak with each of you." Bill walked away, heading for a patrol officer. The man nodded before he headed for his vehicle, leaving to do what Bill had requested of him.

Nollan roused at last, finding Michael standing beside him.

"Nollan? What did you go and do?" Michael had been worried when Richard had called him, despite Richard's reassurances.

"I have no idea. Get me out of here. I need to find Naomi." Nollan fought against Michael's hand on his shoulder. "If you don't help me, I'm walking out of here."

"I know that you are. Bill asked that we wait for him. He wants to talk with you."

"That's not happening." In spite of the dizziness that hit him as he rose, Nollan was on his feet, heading for the ambulance bay doors and leaving. Michael was beside him, stopping as Nollan stopped. "I don't have a vehicle."

"I do. This way. I don't like that you're doing this, Richard but I understand why. Let's get you home."

Two hours later, Michael looked up to find Nollan sleeping in his chair. He rose to cover his cousin with a blanket before heading for the kitchen. He didn't know what number that cup of coffee was but he needed another one. A knock at the door sent him heading that way.

"Richard? You're here?" Michael stepped back to let Richard enter.

"I am. Where's Nollan?"

"In the living room. He's sleeping. And you should be too." Michael headed back towards the kitchen. "I have coffee if that helps."

"It does. I need your help."

"Me? I'm not in law enforcement." Michael's face showed his surprise.

"I know that you're not. But you know what your father teaches. You know your cousin. I need information on how that goes with this." Richard slapped his copy of the notes at Michael's chest.

Michael's hand reached for them, barely managing to capture them before they fluttered to the floor.

"What's this?" Michael was confused.

"This is what Nollan has discovered. We need to tie it all together. Whoever it is has taken Naomi, it was done likely to force Nollan into something. We just don't know what that something is."

"And you think that I might be able to put it all together for you? Let me read it over. I'll call Dad later to get his feeling on that man." He caught Richard's look of surprise. "Yes, Nollan has talked to me about him. We need to find him. I don't know that Naomi will live if we don't."

"That's our fear, Michael. We fear that if Nollan doesn't cooperate, they will kill Naomi. And he will put himself out there to save her,"

"I know that he will. And that would mean he will die." Michael grew quiet as he read through the paperwork, leaning against the kitchen counter.

Richard watched him, knowing that he had taken a step that he usually didn't. He had brought in a civilian to the investigation. He began to pray for Naomi, just asking for the Lord to protect her. His thought was that if they didn't find her soon, that they would never find her.

Michael looked up at last, his thoughts muddled. He had to think this through. This kind of thinking he did best by pacing. He paced, thinking through the conclusions that Nollan had arrived at. He nodded at

last, heading for Nollan. He needed his cousin awake
to talk with him and talk over what he himself had
concluded.

———

Chapter 40

Naomi continued to fight her abductor, even in the vehicle. Her eyes were watering from the chemicals in the smoke. That did not stop her. He made no effort to bind her. Instead, cold gray eyes filled with hatred and anger glittered at her through the respirator mask that he wore. Naomi blinked rapidly to clear the tears from her eyes.

The vehicle came to a stop on the other side of town in front of a beautiful, well-maintained house. Naomi stared at it, her mind working rapidly. She knew that if she ended up inside it, she not likely would come out. At least, that was her thought. And if she did come out, it would more than likely be in a body bag. Hearing the lock click, Naomi shoved at her door and sprang from the car, her feet taking her at a rapid pace away from the car.

She could hear the shouts of the men behind her and then the sound of their pounding feet. Her own feet picked up their pace. Her head was moving from side to side, desperate to find somewhere to hide. She ducked down a driveway and ran for the backyard of a house, through it and then through the yard of the house behind it. Naomi slid to a stop before she was running back towards that area, knowing that if she could make it to an adjacent street, she would be able to find sanctuary at a friend's house.

Naomi's breath was coming in gasps. Her legs were tiring as she approached the house, her eyes on the street. She didn't see or hear the men but she was not fooled. They would be out there. Heading for the back of the house, she searched for the key. Finding it, her hand reached for it. She paused, a frown on her face, before she was on her feet once more. No, Naomi was not going to go in there. God was stopping her from that. She was on the move again, this time away from the house and towards the downtown.

The men searched for Naomi, not wanting to admit to their employee that she had disappeared. They were still in shock that she had and somewhat in awe that she had been able to. They returned to their vehicle, driving around the neighbourhood, still not finding her. The loud and angry arguments broke out between them, with the driver turning at last towards Richard's home. The vehicle slowed as it passed the house, the men watching the activity going on there and the red and blue emergency lights flashing across the scene. This drive did not stop the argument waging inside the car.

Naomi paused her run at last, leaning against a building in the downtown area, a hand to her chest to help try and ease her breathing. She jumped as she felt a hand on her arm, her eyes huge with fear as she twisted quickly to face the person who stood nearby. Old George was there, simply taking her arm and leading her towards a building where he knew that she would be safe.

"Naomi? What did you go and do?" Old George dropped the act that he was usually in, straightening up and going into full police mode.

"I was kidnapped, Old George. God allowed me to escape but they are searching for me. Someone gassed us while we were at Richard's house. I don't know how Nollan, Richard, and Don are. And I need to reach out to Bill." Naomi paced, not comfortable where she was but also knowing that she was safe for the moment.

Old George nodded. He had just heard on the streets that someone was after Naomi. He had been surprised to see her in the downtown area and running at that. He reached into his stash of food, handing her a bottle of water.

"Sit, Naomi. I'll get word to either Bill or Lily. They'll come for you." Old George moved away, the phone that he kept secreted in his clothing pulled out so that he could make a call.

Bill answered his call, somewhat surprised that Old George was calling him.

"Bill, don't speak. This is quick. I have Naomi hidden away. She's managed to escape and ran."

Bill breathed a sigh of relief. Naomi was safe. Now, they just had to find her kidnappers and then solve this. This was getting old, he decided. He wanted it to stop. His friends had suffered enough. He knew only too well how that felt. Losing his young bride when they had only been married for six months was a hurt that had taken time to heal. Having Cora back in his life and as his wife had been a blessing that God had given them both.

Richard walked towards him, Don at his side. Both men had refused to be taken to the hospital. Don had found Richard later that day and then both had gone to find Bill.

"Bill, what now? How do we find Naomi?" Richard was more worried than he wanted to admit. Don's hand rested on his shoulder for a moment.

"She's safe, Richard. I just heard from someone. She managed to get away and ran. I would like to know how she did that."

Richard breathed a sigh of relief. That was one thing that they didn't have to worry about now. Whoever Naomi was with was known to Bill. Bill would not be that confident in her safety if it was something other than that.

"Now, we need to pull in and solve this. We were working through more information with Michael. He's reaching out to his father."

"That's good. For now, I need to head for where Naomi is. I'll bring her to Nollan's. Head back that way."

Bill walked away, the men's eyes following him.

"It has to be someone undercover for Bill to be that calm." Don's statement was confident.

"I suspect that it is. Listen, you need to head out. Thanks for coming, Don. I'm sorry that it ended this way."

Don shrugged, knowing that was one of the hazards of their work

"It is what it is, Richard. Take care."

Michael looked around as Nollan finally appeared, ragged in his appearance. He simply shoved his cousin into a chair and slapped a mug of coffee in front of him.

Nollan nodded slowly, not quite sure what had happened.

"Michael? Any word on Naomi yet?"

"She's safe, Nollan. Richard is on his way back here. He stopped to find Bill who told him that she was safe."

Nollan breathed a sigh of relief. Now, he could continue his search for the man without worrying about his lady.

Chapter 41

Naomi slipped away from Old George and headed for her home. He had walked her to her home, waiting until after dark to do so. She locked the back door behind her, turning on only a few low lights. Reaching for her phone, she sent off a quick message to Richard. She didn't know if he would get it or not. He responded quickly, advising her that the three men were safe.   Naomi drew in a quick breath of relief. Now, she could relax to a certain extent.

Rubbing at her wet hair after her shower, Naomi popped two pieces of bread into the toaster. She needed to eat but wasn't that hungry. She was determined to solve the mystery and solve it that night.

Nollan turned as he heard Richard speaking to him. It took him a moment to focus on the other man.

"You said something, Richard?"

"I did, Nollan. You need to get some rest." Richard's hand rested on Nollan's shoulder. "We'll get Naomi here with you tomorrow. For tonight, I'm with you. Bill had a patrol officer parked outside. Naomi's safe for the night."

Nollan nodded, heading for his bed. He couldn't focus or think straight at the moment. He would have to leave it all with God. There was just no other option.

Bill found Old George in Ev's diner, sliding into a seat across from him. He nodded as the server approached. He would get the dinner special, and that was just all right with him.

"Old George? She's safe?" Bill's voice was very low, barely audible.

"She is. She's home. She'll be heading towards Nollan tomorrow."

Bill thanked the server for his dinner, his head bowing over it for a moment. He ate in silence, his thoughts troubled for a moment.

"I'll find her in the morning. We need to get the two together." Bill knew that Richard was planning on staying with Nollan tonight. We need you to come on in soon."

Old George nodded, knowing that he would need to. He just wasn't sure that he wanted to. He liked the freedom of what he did now.

"We'll see, Bill." Old George hesitated before he spoke. "Watch Nollan. Someone is really desperate to get to him." He slid an envelope across the table. "This is what I was offered. I said no. It's up to you to find this man." He was gone before Bill could speak.

Bill finished his meal, tucked the envelope into a pocket, paid for the meal, and walked out. He headed for the office, knowing that Andrew would still be there. He needed to be in on whatever decision was made.

Andrew looked up from the piece of paper. He shook his head. This was not who he had expected, but thinking it through, he nodded.

"Bill? Where do we stand with the investigation?"

"The man who set the bombs? We've arrested him. He was the student in Naomi's class. Justin Everett. He is not talking. He's scared of someone. And I think that someone is that person who approached Old George."

"What about his family? How far does it go?"

"His father is part of that company who disappeared. Justin was the CEO of it. From what others we've arrested have said, he made the move of contacting Nollan. What his plans were, that's what we working through."

"I see. And the other company?"

"It's owned by the same numbered company. Emma searching that through for us. Samuel's dad, Barnabas, is working on the finances. He sent an email to Lily. I haven't spoken to her as yet. She was off today."

Andrew's gaze centred on the wall across from him. He wanted this over for Naomi and Nollan. Yet there was still work to do.

"How do you plan on working this, Bill?"

"I think they'll go on the offensive. Naomi's not one to sit back and wait. Nollan is hurting in many ways. He wants this over. They're a couple, you know." He grinned as Andrew laughed. "Richard has called in his team to work on it tomorrow. They've done a lot all ready."

Bill walked away at that. He had work to do. It was coming to a head, he thought, and he needed to be ready.

———

Naomi opened the door the next morning, finding Timothy standing there. She didn't say anything, just grabbed what she needed and walked out with him. She had no idea where she was heading. She just prayed that she would be with Nollan.

"Timothy? How is everyone from yesterday?" Naomi's voice was worried.

"They're all fine. Nollan was hit the hardest. Richard says he's better this morning. We're heading for Nollan's place."

"I wondered where we were heading. I'm glad. How close are we to solving this?"

"Close, I think. Richard spoke with Bill this morning. They're making arrests and closing in on the head one. He's thinking that it will be in the next day or so. For now, we keep working and funneling what we find on to Bill or Lily. Emma's weighing in as well."

"I thought that she would." Naomi stared at Nollan's house as Timothy parked. "Timothy, how did you do it at this point?"

"How did I do it? Prayer, Naomi. That's what got me through. That and the support of all of you and everyone else. Knowing that God was protecting us? That is so important to us. He doesn't leave us or forget about us. That promise is what helps."

"It does." Naomi made no move to open the truck door. She was unsure of herself, something totally out of character for her. How did she go forward?

Chapter 42

Nollan looked around that afternoon as he heard Bill's voice, rising to his feet as Bill approached them. He felt Naomi's hand on his back and simply reached to wrap her close to him.

"Bill? You're here? I don't if that is good or bad." Nollan caught the movement of the others as they gathered around them.

"It's over, Nollan and Naomi. We have everyone this time with our arrests. We have the head one. There is no one else. We'll meet in a few days. Thank you for all your work."

Nollan's knees gave way as he realized that the danger was over. He felt Naomi's arms hugging him. He reached for her, hugging her back.

Richard walked away, his emotions overcoming him for a moment. He could hear the conversation behind him, relief the uppermost emotion that he could hear. His eyes searched the sky, his heart full of gratitude to their heavenly Father.

Naomi walked her house late that night. She had been in contact with her family, who had rejoiced with her. Nollan had driven her home, reluctant to leave her but knowing that now they could move forward with what they were looking to in their lives.

Nollan handed his cousin a mug of coffee before he lifted his own, sipping at it as he studied his cousin.

"It's really over, Nollan?" Michael was hopeful that it was.

"Bill tells us that it is. I pray that he is right. I don't think we can do more than we have. It's taken a toll on all of us."

"Mom and Dad were happy to hear that. When are we meeting with Bill?" Michael grinned at his cousin.

"I think on Saturday. I'll host a meal for us. Bill was agreeable to that."

Saturday found the group gathered at Nollan's. He watched his family as they mingled with Naomi and her family and her team mates. She was glowing, he decided, more beautiful than ever. Michael stood beside him, his eyes on his cousin.

"How are you doing, Nollan? I mean, really." Michael waited for his cousin to respond, content for the moment to be with his family.

"Me? I'm doing okay, I think. It will take some time to get back to where I was. I wouldn't want to go through this again. That's a fact." He grinned at Michael, his arm reaching out to sweep Naomi to his side, causing her to blush as he did so.

Bill stood for a moment, Andrew at one side of him, and Lily on his other side. *For once,* he thought, *we were able to solve this without one final bit of danger for the couple. Now, to put it all together for them. It really didn't make much sense to me, he thought, but then it not always does. I am just glad that God was there and protected them.*

"Bill? What can you tell us?" Nollan's voice sounded loud in the sudden silence. He winced, Naomi's around him tightening a bit as she smothered a giggle. He smiled down at her, neither seeing the looks of happiness that were sent their way.

"What can I tell you?" Bill shook a finger at Nollan. "I'm still stunned to some degree as to why this happened. At first glance, it didn't make much sense to us, but when those who were involved began to talk, then it came together.

"The student from your class, Jake, had fixated on Naomi just because she had such good marks. He got good marks in many classes when he shouldn't have. How? His father bought them. We have been in touch with the college. We are not sure if anything can be done at this point. Jake, you refused the bribe. His father said that it was never offered as a bribe to you but as a suggestion. You refused to even let him finish what he wanted. That caused his father, Dustin, to be incensed with you. He felt that you were denying his son the life that he deserved.

"He had the two companies that you flagged, Nollan. His son was put in as CEO of the first one that you first flagged. There wasn't any work being done there. They were fishing, as they said, to try and bring you down. You had stopped a friend of theirs from putting a product on the market that would have caused multiple deaths. I don't think that you would have even connected the two friends.

"For some reason, they connected you two. Justin has said that they realized that you were a nephew to Jake and Maggie. They had observed that

Naomi was in the tea room a lot and decided that you were friends. That backfired on them. Dustin and Justin are the ones who arranged for the bombings, the gas attack, the assaults. It was done to discredit you both. And if you were harmed or killed in the process, that would have been all right with them. It still is not clear how they thought this would discredit you.”

Nollan nodded, knowing what he had found what he could. He also knew that there were facts that Bill could not tell them.

Naomi moved around Nollan’s house after everyone had left. She loved the house even more than her own home. Nollan watched her before he moved towards her, wrapping her into a hug before he kissed her.

“Thank you, Naomi. You and your friends helped solve this.”

Naomi grinned up at him, her face glowing with happiness.

“You as well. You started it all, you know.”

Nollan began to laugh, seeing the mirth sparkling in her eyes.

“I guess, in a way, I did. If I had not, I would not have met you. My life would be empty.”

“As would mine. I need to head out, Nollan. You’re picking me up in the morning for church and taking me out to lunch.” She smirked as she headed for her car, hearing his laughter floating behind her as he followed her.

———

Six months later, Naomi walked the path in the park that she favoured. She was happy. She enjoyed the training that they were doing much more than she thought that she would. Nollan was a big part of her life now. *Thank you, Lord. You protected us, just as You have promised. You have brought peace to us. I love this man in my life. I didn't think that I would have anyone. Yet, you planned ahead of time for this. Bless the life that we are thinking about building together. Love you, Lord.*

Naomi turned as she heard a whistle, a praise chorus from Sunday wafting through the air. Nollan was walking towards her, his arms open as she ran towards him, confident in her greeting and welcome.

Kissing her, Nollan stared down at her upturned face. He loved her, he knew, more and more each day. He thanked God daily for bringing her into his life.

"Nollan? You're here!"

"I am. It didn't take as long as I thought it would out of town. I think that I am on the right track with this new work."

"I think that you are. Working towards disease prevention is where your heart is." Naomi reached for his hand, leading him towards their favourite bench near the river's edge.

Nollan sat, drawing her down beside him. He wrapped an arm around her. She had become important to his family just as he had to hers. Her father had approached him the week before, asking him what his intentions were. He had grinned at Nollan, knowing that Nollan wouldn't say. Nollan had grinned back, simply stating that Naomi needed and deserved to hear from him first before anyone else. Benjamin grinned back, admitting that Nollan was right. He had stood, welcomed Nollan to the family, and then walked away.

Biting at his lip for a moment, Nollan hesitated to speak. He had had a speech all memorized. The ring was buttoned in his shirt pocket. It had belonged to his mother, a family heirloom that he hoped Naomi would wear. They had spent many hours sharing about their families. Naomi was saddened that Nollan's parents were not there but had gladly shared her family with him.

Naomi was quiet. It had been a busy day for her and she was tired. She rested back against Nollan, content to sit and watch the traffic on the paths around them. She turned her face up to him, finding his eyes on her.

"Naomi, you are a beautiful lady who I am blessed to call my best friend. I love you, sweetheart. We have not known each other for years. What we went through brought us closer to one another and quicker than if we had known each other for years. Will you be mine for life, my helpmeet, my best friend, the one who God planned for me to be with?"

Naomi blinked against the tears that gathered. She nodded, unable to speak for a moment. She swallowed hard.

"I love you too, Nollan. Yes, I will marry you. What you said? Ditto." She smiled as Nollan laughed.

"Don't ever lose your sense of humour, sweetheart. It gets you through the hard stuff." He unbuttoned his shirt pocket and pulled out the ring. "This ring belonged to my Mom. It's a family heirloom. I would be honoured if you would wear it." He held the blue diamond ring, waiting until she nodded, and then slipped it on her slender finger. It fit perfectly.

Naomi stirred at last, knowing that they would need to head off soon.

"Bill called me this morning." Naomi had not been surprised to hear from him. "He said that they all took plea deals. The evidence was just too strong."

"I wondered. He told me that would likely be the case. I'm okay with that. I was not looking forward to testifying. Neither were you. I have no idea what their sentences will be."

"Nor do I. I'm glad that their companies are closed. It scared me when you told me what the effects could be."

"Me, too." On his feet, he tugged her to her feet and then walked back towards his truck. Tucking her inside, he looked up, seeing the first stars of the night. His eyes followed the shooting star, a wish coming to his mind. *Thank You, Lord, for my lady. And thank You for who You are.*

Dear Readers:

Thanks you for choosing Naomi and Nollan's story. It was once again not quite the story as I envisioned it. Unruly characters just walk in, take over, and tell their own story. It was an interesting one as it unfolded.

God does protect us, in so many ways. Many times, we not likely even know when he protected us. He also brings people into our lives that may or may not impact us in a definite way. That is what happened with these two.

Once more, Abe and his team appeared. Their stories are in the *His Guardians* series. Bill and Cora's story is *Hidden in the Hollow*. Andrew and Phoebe's story is *The Potter's Hands*. Samuel and Adam and those friends have their stories in *His Warriors*. Silas and Madigan's story is *Strong Courage*.

As we make our way through life, it is easy to step away from God, to think that we can do so much better than Him at taking care of ourselves. That is not true. As believers, we need to remember that He will never leave us, never turn His back on us, and always welcomes us back when we stray. My father always referred to the times that we stray as being in the desert (just as the Israelites were for so many years). He was a wise man who taught me much about the Bible without saying many words. I miss his wisdom and I miss my Mom's prayers.

God bless each one of you.

Ronna

Website: ronnabacon.com

9 781999 882109